JASMINE

THE WAITE FAMILY SERIES

BOOK 5

KATHI S. BARTON

This is a work of fiction. Names, characters, places, and incidents are products of the author's imagination or are used fictitiously and are not to be construed as real. Any resemblance to actual events, locations, organizations, or person, living or dead, is entirely coincidental.

World Castle Publishing, LLC
Pensacola, Florida
Copyright © Kathi S. Barton 2013
Print ISBN: 9781938961748
eBook ISBN: 9781938961755
First Edition World Castle Publishing, LLC January 1, 2013
http://www.worldcastlepublishing.com
Licensing Notes
Cover: Karen Fuller
Photos: Shutterstock
Editor: Brieanna Robertson

Chapter 1

Jazzie watched as Nathan came toward her. She'd been sitting in this stupid office chair for more than two hours waiting for someone to come and relieve her. When she'd volunteered to help out at the office for Payton she'd thought it would be fun. But it was really boring.

"I didn't know you were here," he told her as soon as he saw her. "I thought Lilliane would be here today."

She could swear that he was looking for a way to escape. It hurt her to know that he avoided her, but she simply smiled at him and pretended that she didn't notice. "Nope, just me. At least for another hour anyway. I have another thing I have to do and told Payton this morning that I could only spare a few hours today." He glanced at the doorway again and she sighed. "Why don't you do whatever it is you need then go, Nathan? You obviously don't want to be here with me."

He looked at her sharply and she stood up and walked out the door he'd been staring at. She thought about telling him to watch the phones, but didn't think she could speak around the lump in her throat. She was nearly to her car when she realized that she'd forgotten her purse. Oh well, there wasn't anything much in it anyway and there was no way she was going back to get it.

Jazzie knew she was in love with Nathan Howard. She'd been nearly there for almost a month, but watching him with Tonya and Connor, her niece and nephew, at Lilliane and Shamus' wedding, she'd taken the tumble. She knew that he thought she was a lazy tease, always seemingly out of work and having fun, but she actually had a good job that paid very well. Well, it paid really well now.

She was Jasmine Blackwell, the bestselling author of the most steamy romance novels ever to hit the market. Or at least that's what one critic had said. Others had said similar things, mostly how her story lines and her characters came alive on the page. She'd cut every one of them out and put them into a notebook. She still couldn't believe that people were actually paying her to read books. She'd always assumed that everyone could write if they wanted and had been surprised when she'd found out that they didn't. Her publisher said some of the mystic surrounding her was that no one knew anything about her. And there had never been a single picture taken of her that would lead anyone to believe she was who she was.

She'd been writing stories in her head since she'd been a kid. Not the sort that she wrote now. Those would have been too much for a kid to deal with. But stories about a little girl who was saved from her mean step parents by a nice rich couple and taken away to live happily ever after.

It wasn't until she got older that she realized a few things. There was no such thing as happily ever after, at least not to her kind, and that no matter how much she wished it, she wasn't her sisters and brother.

She loved them dearly. All of them. Cain, her brother, made her feel like she could do anything she wanted, but she couldn't. Not really. There were times when she knew he despaired of her ever being anything more than a flighty woman without direction, but she'd proven, maybe not to him but to herself, that she could do one thing and do it very well. And every time one of her royalty checks came in the mail she knew there were a few others out there that liked what she did as well. She pulled up in front of her little house and got out. Her cell phone was ringing when she got inside.

It was Nathan. She'd given him her number once so that if he ever needed a friend to talk to he could feel free to call her. This was the first time he'd ever actually used it. She put it on the counter and set about pulling out what she needed to make a salad. It wasn't until she was finishing up her lunch when she realized he'd left her a message.

She debated on just leaving it until she was in a better frame of mind. But then she realized that that might be a long time from now. She dialed her voicemail as she walked to her office and unlocked the door. By the time she was sitting at her desk, his voice came across the line.

"I wasn't trying to get away from you. What a silly thing to…why did you say that? I have never tried to get away…Jazzie, I would like for you to call me back. We need to straighten this out immediately."

She laughed out loud at his tone. He sounded like he was upset with her. She was smiling when she brought up the first of three books she was planning on working on today. There was no way she was calling him back. She had things to do and they didn't involve trying to tangle through the mess that was Nathan Howard.

She was deep into the plot of the second book when she realized that someone was laying on her doorbell. She pulled up the monitor on her computer screen and groaned when she saw who it was. She'd almost take Nathan over her mother right now. Jazzie thought about ignoring the demand, but realized that even if she wanted to her mother would wait her out and pounce on her when she had to go outside.

She opened the door, but didn't take the chain off. Her mother frowned at her when she didn't open the door all the way for her. Jazzie had too much going on right now to fuck with Guinevere Waite.

"I want you to open this door, young lady. I would like to have a conversation with you and I am not going to do so in the doorway." She actually took a step forward as if Jazzie would comply. "Now, Jasmine. I've been out all day and I want you to make me some dinner and put me up for the night."

"No, Mother. I told you at Lilliane's wedding that until you make it right by her, you and I are through. I told you this the day before yesterday and, again, yesterday." Jazzie started to push the door closed when her mother pushed back.

"You can't expect me to like that gimp, do you? I mean, what if he breeds with her and she has a gimpy baby? Why how will anyone expect me to love it if—"

"First of all, Shamus was shot. He was injured in his leg by a madwoman who took him to try and lure Lilliane to him. Second…you know, I don't give a shit if you understand the difference between being born with a defect and having one forced on you. And I'm certainly not going to explain to you that as her mother, you should love who she loves regardless of what he looks like."

"Oh don't be ridiculous. Who on earth would expect me to love a deformity like that?" Guinevere stomped her foot. "Open this door, Jasmine, or so help me, I'll make you suffer with the likes you've never imagined."

Fear rippled down Jazzie's spine. It was there so quickly and with so much force that she nearly did open the door. But just as she was pushing the door closed to slide the chain, she stiffened. She wasn't a child anymore and she could certainly decide who did or didn't come into her house. So instead of pulling the door open and telling her mother to go away again, she closed the door and turned the lock. She was nearly to her office again when she heard the doorbell sounding.

She sat down hard. And once there she had to bend at the waist and put her head between her knees. She kept telling herself that she wouldn't throw up, she wouldn't throw up until the feeling started to recede. She wasn't herself completely, but she did feel a little less sick to her stomach by the time she sat back up. And, thank you very much, the doorbell was silent.

The memory that had caused her to fear her mother was right there now. Jazzie had tried her very best to forget the nights when she'd been a child. Her father was an abusive man, more than abusive; he'd been damn right sadistic. There were times growing up that Jazzie had wondered if he'd kill her.

But the night that she had been held her down while he…he'd raped her had been what had caused her to fear the dark.

She'd been seventeen. Not a great age for a kid like her. She wasn't as pretty as her sisters, especially not as lovely as the twins, Sin and Lilliane, but she could hold her own in looks. What had set her apart of the other teenagers was that they all thought her odd. She supposed she was. She liked to have fun and she didn't really need a lot of people around to do so.

Quinn and Cain had already moved out, Gracie was in her senior year of high school, and she was a sophomore. The twins, Sin and Lilliane, were still in junior high. She'd been studying for a test the next morning when her mother had knocked on her door. She'd thought that weird as she'd never done it before, but didn't really think anything about it at the time.

"Hello, Jazzie. Your sisters are out on the town. You should have gone with them." Jazzie remembered that her mother sounded funny, her voice slightly higher pitched.

And when she got closer to the bed where Jazzie was sitting she realized something else. It wasn't her mother.

The woman that had entered the room looked like her mother. The hair was different, the same color she thought, but styled differently. Where her mother had always worn hers in a tight bun at the back of her head this woman had hers down and curled. Her father coming into the room and removing his belt made her shift her attention to him rather than try and figure out who the woman was.

She tried to think quickly. She'd didn't think she'd forgotten to do her chores and she knew that she'd not been in trouble at school lately. She did cover for Sin once, took back a library book that was overdue and conned the woman into not charging her any fees, but she was sure that wasn't it. She tossed her books to the floor and tried to get to the closet to lock herself in.

The month before, Cain had installed the lock. There was a latch at the bottom of the door they all knew about but had yet to use. She was nearly there when she felt the first lash of his belt land across her back. She went down quickly.

She could only reason that she'd hit her head. She didn't remember being put on the bed. She certainly would have fought more had she known. She also wouldn't have let them tie her legs to the bottom of the bed and gag her. The woman was at her head, her father at the foot. All her attention was centered on him and not what the woman was saying to her. Not until she realized that she was telling her father how much he was going to enjoy this.

"You fuck that pretty pussy and I swear to you, Roscoe, I'll give you the blow job of your life. That wife of yours will never give you anything like I can do with my mouth."

Jazzie closed her eyes and tried to will her father to go away, to stop what he was doing. She begged the woman to shut the hell up and leave her alone. But he didn't and neither did the woman. Then when he'd finished...finished

10

hurting her, they'd left her there. Left her tied to the bed until her mother had come in.

She had blamed Jazzie for it. Guinevere had slapped her so many times that Jazzie had become dizzy. It wasn't until her mother had worn herself out that Guinevere had told her that if she told one person what had happened, told one single lie about what her father had done, she'd make her suffer with the likes she'd never imagined.

When her phone rang again, this time a tone that made her smile, she got up to go to the kitchen. She grabbed up the phone and was giggling when she said hello to her sister Gracie.

~~~

"I'm sending you something for your birthday. I designed this creation and as soon as it was done I thought, this is so Jazzie." Grace waited for her sister to comment. When she didn't right away she got worried. "What's happened? Did Mother do something to you? That stupid bitch needs to mind her own fucking business."

Gracie heard her sister sob. She wished she could go to her, comfort her in some way, but she knew that she couldn't. She couldn't move back home because of her secret. One that would make them all hate her forever.

"She's not the only one. I was...why do you think Nathan hates me? I've never done anything wrong to him." A short bark of laughter had Gracie smile. "Okay, maybe I have given him one or two reasons to be upset with me. But the guy is too stiff for words."

"And you're in love with him." Jazzie started to stutter, but Gracie cut her off. "You can try and deny it all you want, but I saw the way you looked at him. Like he was a pound of dark chocolate and you were PMSing."

"He doesn't like me," Jazzie said softly. "He avoids me and, just this morning, he accidentally came into the office where I was and he practically trembled in fear I'd do something to him."

"Have you told him how you feel?" As soon as she laughed again, this one bitter and hard, Gracie knew that she hadn't. "You should just tell him. Or jump his bones. I'm pretty sure that'll make him notice you."

"Yeah, I'm sure he'll run for the hills too. I can't do that to Alyssa. She and her brother are making great headway into becoming family again. No, I'm thinking I'm going to just stop going by the office and hide out at my house."

After telling her sister when she'd be shipping out her package they hung up. Gracie wondered long after she'd gone home if her sister would be able to keep away from Nathan Howard. He seemed to be a man who didn't think he was good enough for anyone, much less her flighty sister.

Chapter 2

Nathan waited for over two hours for Miss Waite to call him back. While he'd been waiting he'd made a list of things to say to her. He was working on the third page when his sister walked in. She seemed to be a little upset. He waited until she made sure her water bottle was safe before he spoke.

"I had a tiff with your sister-in-law. She seems to be under the misimpression that I avoid her." Alyssa, apparently satisfied with her bottle, opened it and took a long drink. "I don't want her to think such things."

"Jazzie, I'm guessing? You do avoid her." She smiled at him before she continued. "She can be a bit much at first, but she sort of grows on you. Would you like me to say something to her? I know that she teases you badly sometimes. But she means well."

He thought about it for all of two seconds. "No, I should. I was making a list. I want us to have a clear picture of where our boundaries are so that we can work together. She makes me...uncomfortable sometimes." It was more than that and he knew it. She made him aware of himself. Not just as a person, but as a man. He'd never had that reaction to another person before, at least not that he knew of. Most of his life had been spent in a blur of drugs and alcohol. Mostly the drugs part, he supposed.

He'd taken his first drink at eight. He and his brother had been wandering around a party that his parents had been giving, bored out of their minds. Robert, his then six-year-old brother, had taken the first drink out of the wine bottle left on the table. He'd told Nathan that he had to get his own. He'd opted for a bottle of scotch.

They had both gotten sick. Very sick, as a matter of fact. Their mother, Shannon Howard, had told them that she hoped they'd learned a lesson and left it at that, but their father, Nathan the third, had taken a different approach. He'd beaten both their asses.

At the time, Nathan had hated the man. He'd had no right to judge them on taking a little drink and had said as much to his uncle Samuel about it. Samuel had agreed and, whenever there was another party or a group of them together, he made sure that his favorite nephews had their own little stash of liquor and that no one found out about it. It was his road to destruction.

By the time he was thirteen he was a drunk. And when alcohol didn't work as well to make him feel good he started on drugs. By the time he'd found out he wasn't Nathan's son and that his uncle was his actual father the man who could have saved him from himself was dead. Nathan, the man who had beaten his bottom on more occasions than not, died and left him to his sister. He was lucky that she was just like her dad.

Alyssa brought him back to the present with a short laugh. "She'll love that. I've never met anyone more afraid of lists than she is. I wonder at times how she gets what she needs at the grocery when she goes. I love her to death, but she is the most scatterbrained woman I've ever meet."

Nathan didn't know why, but he had a feeling that Miss Waite was a lot smarter than anyone was giving her credit for. He didn't say that to his sister, but he thought Jasmine

14

might need to be watched a bit closer. He only nodded and added one more thing to his list.

"I was wondering if I could talk to you about the project we discussed the other day? I was wondering if you've given it any more thought." He wanted to take on the library project with all his heart, but he didn't want to fail his sister. "I have some more numbers for you, if that helps."

"I looked over what you gave me the other week. I think it's a great idea. But I only have one issue." He felt his heart thud. Here it came; she was going to tell him that she'd decided on someone else to head the project. "You'll have to have a staff and an office. I hate that I don't have the room for you on this floor. Do you think you could see your way to have your office up here and the staff on the lower floor? At least until your building is completed?"

He was so ready to tell her that he'd help whoever she'd picked out to head it that it took him several moments to realize what she'd said. He could only stare at her as she waited for his answer. He asked her to repeat it.

"I want you to stay on the top floor with me. I love having you close at hand and Connor knows that all he needs to do is toddle down to find you. I think he'll miss you being where he can find you too. Especially if you take your drawer of little cars from him."

"You're letting me do it?" His voice squeaked with pleasure. "I don't know what...thank you, Alyssa. I won't let you down. My office? You want..." Nathan took a deep breath before continuing. "Your dad used to have them in is drawers, you know. The cars. He would give me one every time I came into his office when I...before I...before I screwed up."

"I know. I found them in his desk after...when I was cleaning things up. And you didn't screw up, Nathan. You were misled and, because of that, you got sidetracked. You're not going back there again so we move on and up,

15

right?" She stood up and went toward the door as she continued. "Connor might not have known *our* dad, Nathan, and he was our dad, but he has you to teach him things that I can't. You're his biggest hero right now and I love you for it."

After she left he reached for his phone. He was going to try and reach Jasmine again, but his office phone rang before he could pull hers up on his cell. He frowned when he saw the number. What could she want?

"Mrs. Waite, what can I do for you? If you're looking for Cain or Alyssa, they are both—"

"What on earth would I want that woman to talk to me for? She would simply hang up on me anyway. No, dear boy, I've called to speak to you." Guinevere Waite was not a nice person and Nathan hated to think what she'd want from him. "I was wondering if you could help me find some drugs. I need something to help me—"

"I don't know anything about drugs, Mrs. Waite. I've...you'll have to see your doctor if there is a problem that you feel is only solved with a pill." He was trembling with the need to slam the phone down on her. "I've been clean for a long while now, as you know."

"Yes, yes, I'm aware of the little party that your...*sister*"—she made it sound like a dirty word—"gave you when you hit your one year mark. Total waste of time and money, if you ask me. You type of people always go back on the sauce. It's only a matter of time before you do. No, I need you to find me something to help me relax. I'm sure you have contacts still. A man like you will need to keep in touch with the lowlifes just to keep your finger in the pot."

Nathan wanted to think she was kidding him. But he knew better. She'd been anything but civil to him and his sister since he'd met her last year. She was never anything but a bitch and right now, he wasn't in the mood to fuck with her.

"How you live with yourself daily is beyond me. You are the most horrid woman I've ever met." He stood up as he felt himself getting more and more pissed. "I will only say this the one time. I do not know any 'lowlifes,' as you put it. Maybe you should look at the people you hang out with before you go pointing your finger at others." He slammed the phone down so hard he felt it vibrate up his arm.

It took him ten minutes to calm himself down and another five before he thought he could drive. He grabbed up his coat and decided he needed a break. Alyssa had a gym put in the offices last year when they'd moved to this newer building and he decided that he could use a good two or three hours down there before he went home. Nathan thought maybe he should invest in one for his house too.

~~~

Drew watched Nathan move from one piece of equipment to the other. The man was going to have a heart attack before the end of the day if he kept this pace up. He'd already done forty minutes on the treadmill and another on the stair machine. If he did that long on the bike, Drew decided that he was going to put the guy up for the next Olympics. He moved over to the bike next to him and handed him a bottle of cool water.

"Drink it slow or you'll get cramps." Nathan nodded but didn't speak. "You want to talk about it?" A grunt was all he got. "Or I could just wait until they rush you to the hospital for heart failure and have the doctor give you something that'll make you talk."

"I don't do drugs anymore," Nathan snarled at him. "And I don't know any fucking lowlifes that I can get any from either. I'm clean, damn it."

Drew nearly laughed, but from the look the other man was giving him he decided he might live longer if he didn't.

17

Instead, he just kept up his own pace with the bike until Nathan started to slow. Before Drew could ask if he wanted to talk about it Nathan stopped moving.

"She said she wanted something to help her relax. I'd like to give her something to relax. A bullet between the eyes comes to mind." Drew didn't say anything as Nathan continued. "She said that the party my sister gave me for my one-year was a waste of money and time. Do you know how much that meant to me to have her do that? Plenty, I can tell you. Then that bitch...how the fuck did she have such wonderful kids and be such a...such a cancer on the earth?"

Nodding his understanding and knowing who Nathan was talking about made Drew wonder the same thing. "Guinevere is something else, you got that right. I take it she's the reason for the hyped up exercise program you're killing yourself over."

"She called right before I left my office. She said that I would be back on the sauce again soon enough." Nathan took another swig of water. "I don't know anyone who could stand to be around her all the time. How do you do it?'

Drew laughed. "I don't. I only talk to her when I need to and have my secretary answer the phone so that I don't have to. I told you to hire one last month. See what I meant by having a built-in call screen?'

"I'm going to do it first thing in the morning," Nathan mumbled. "I'll have to hurry or I'll be wearing out the equipment down here."

Both men went to the shower, cleaned up, and changed. Drew was glad that his boss and sister-in-law had decided that having private showers instead of open ones when he stepped in the bath and saw Allen Davidson there. The man would come down for about ten minutes and work out then hang around the shower room until someone came in he could invite to dinner. Plus, the man had to weigh all of four hundred pounds, not a sight that Drew wanted to see naked.

18

He was dressed and waiting for Nathan twenty minutes later after assuring Allen that he and Nathan had a business dinner they had to go to.

The two men did end up at The Court of Small Clams together. And business was the furthest thing from either of their minds. Drew suggested they call the other men, Shamus and Payton, who asked if they could bring along Cain to round out the night. They were just getting their salads set before them when Drew mentioned Guinevere.

"She actually called you to ask for…I don't know why I'm surprised. Not about her calling you, because I can't tell you enough how sorry I am she did that, but trying to get something illegal. I refused to give her anything stronger when she came by my office last week," Cain said as he took a pull on his beer. "She said she was having problems sleeping in that 'horrid house' I'd put her in. Do you know how much I could get for that house on the open market right now?"

Drew answered for him. "One point three million. I know, I had to have it appraised for you last year. I'm sorry to say this, Cain, because I know she's your mom, but she's nuts. And Nathan came down to the gym while I was there to burn off some of her nastiness."

It was well after midnight when the men went their separate ways. Drew could tell that Nathan had something on his mind. The man had checked his cell phone several times before they'd left. He wondered if it was a girl and decided that he hoped so. Nathan was too nice of a guy not to have a bevy of women hanging around. Drew crawled into bed with his wife and thought this was the way to be, happily married, with children sleeping just down the hall from them.

Chapter 3

"This is going to be huge, you know that don't you? My goodness, Jazzie, where do you come up with these story lines? If this series sells anything like the last one did you're going to be big."

Jazzie only listened to her publisher with half an ear. She was still in the middle of the book she'd had to leave when she'd been summoned to this luncheon with Chastity Midland. She wouldn't have come, but the woman said she had something big to share.

"I know. My last royalty check was big enough that I could pay for my house. Next I want a new car, so I hope you're right." Jazzie had put the house in her pen name and they all thought she was renting the house she'd moved into six months ago. "I have to get something more reliable before winter."

Chastity didn't say anything, for which Jazzie was glad. Chastity couldn't understand why her bestselling author didn't just go and apply for a loan to get what she wanted and Jazzie couldn't make her understand that she was too afraid to get into debt. If she couldn't pay for it when she wanted it, then she simply saved until she could. It was that simple.

Even with the success of her books she was afraid that people would suddenly figure out who she was and stop buying them. Then she would be in hock to her ass. No, her way was better for her. Every time she got a check she was amazed. It blew her away to see that people were actually putting out money to buy her books.

"You said you had some good news. Please tell me that that guy at the office has finally asked you out? That's wonderful news." Jazzie frowned when Chastity laughed and said no. "Then what? I really need to get back. I left Devin tied up on the bed and his girlfriend trying out some nipple clamps on him."

"Oh my, I can't wait to read that one. No, this is about the Montgomery Series you wrote. I have someone who wants to make it into a movie." Chastity handed her a thick contract as she continued. "They said they want to start putting out the feelers for actors right away. There was talk from him that that Bacon woman has already agreed to do the...are you all right, love?"

No, she wasn't. A movie deal? She was just getting used to people buying her books. How was she supposed to deal with people watching it on the big screen? Jazzie picked up her glass of water and drained it. Then reached for her tea to do the same. She was dizzy and scared and nervous all at the same time. She felt the air in the room smother her. She knew that at any moment she was going to pass out when, suddenly, she was looking at the floor and someone was pressing her head down.

"Stay there, damn it. What the hell is wrong with you anyway?" She tried to sit up, but Nathan pressed her back. "I said to stay there."

"You can't expect me to answer your stupid question if my head is between my legs. Let me up, damn it, I'm fine." He let her up slowly, but didn't move away when she was upright. "I'm fine. Now go back to whatever you were doing and leave me be."

"I was leaving when I heard this woman"—he nodded toward Chastity—"shout your name. And there you were wilting like a hot-house flower. What did you do, skip breakfast?"

"No, I did not skip breakfast. She and I were talking about something and I had a slight…fright. But I'm better now so go away." She looked over at her publisher when she cleared her throat.

"I'm Chastity Midland. I'm a very close friend of Jazzie's. And you would be?" Jazzie was suddenly glad she'd asked her publisher to never ever, ever tell anyone who she was.

"Leaving," Jazzie said as she turned her back on Nathan. "I'm sure you have plenty of things to do outside of this building."

She wasn't really surprised when he took Chastity's hand and kissed it before telling her his name, but nothing could have prepared her for him pulling out a chair and sitting at their table. She looked at him shocked, and he simply winked at Chastity.

"She doesn't like me even though I just saved her from falling on her face in a very busy restaurant." He started to pick up the contract she'd laid on the table when she'd gotten scared.

Jazzie snatched it from him with a glare. "Do you mind? I am in the middle of something here and it doesn't involve you."

He took the contract back and had it open before she could get it. She tried to get it back, but he must have read some of it before he looked at her. His face might have been funny if she wasn't sure he'd read enough to figure out just what the contract was about. He flipped through a few more pages before he set it back down on the table.

"I thought it was a job offer or something. I had…how long?" She didn't answer so he turned to Chastity. "How long have you been working for her?"

Jazzie had to hand it to Chastity, she didn't say anything. She did, however, gather up her things to go. She had her jacket on and the check in her hand before she looked at both of them.

"You two work this out. Jazz, I told you this would happen sooner or later." She picked up the contract and handed it to her. "Read this over and let me know by Monday. I have an appointment with the head of HBO on Wednesday. That way, if there are things you want to change, we still have time to do so. Mr. Howard, it was very nice meeting you." Then she breezed out of the restaurant.

Jazzie leaned over to pick up her purse. She still had the contract in her hand and was just about ready to stand when he put his hand on her arm and held her there. Before she could tell him to back the fuck off he spoke.

"You obviously don't want anyone to know what you're doing in your spare time, so either sit down and tell me or I'll call your family and tell them. Though why you don't want them to know is beyond me."

"They wouldn't care." He snorted at her answer. "Well, they wouldn't. I don't most of the time. What do you want? Money? I assure you, I don't have any. And besides, blackmail is against the law."

"I'm well aware of the law. And I'm sure you're wrong about your family." He nodded toward the contract again. "Are you going to tell them about that? It seems like a huge deal."

She shoved the contract in her bag before turning back to him. "No. You didn't answer me. What do you want?"

He smiled at the waitress when she came by. He ordered them both some pie. She loved cherry pie and didn't know

24

what to think when he ordered himself a slice of apple too. When she was gone, he looked at her.

"I don't want anything. I'm just a little…are you aware that Alyssa and Quinn read your books? I'm assuming they're your books and that you're Jasmine Blackwell. Just last week I overheard them talking about the newest… You were there too. Yet you didn't tell them. Why?"

She squirmed in her seat. She felt her face heat with embarrassment. She looked around the other tables, wondering if anyone could hear them. This was why she had a strict policy about anyone knowing who she was. It embarrassed her. "I like my private life. And besides, they wouldn't believe me anyway. I don't most of the time." She glanced down at her bag. "I *really* don't believe that."

He laughed and she was surprised by it. He rarely laughed around her and she thought he had such a great laugh, too. Their pie arrived, as did coffee for him. She got a refill on her tea and they ate their dessert in silence.

"I take it you don't do book signings either." She shook her head at his observation. "So, who besides your lovely publisher knows besides me now?"

She tried to ignore the hurt of him thinking Chastity was lovely. "No one. Not even the people in her office know. Chastity and I talk almost every day so if you want her phone number I'm sure I can give it to you."

He didn't say anything and she made a mental note to ask Chastity if she could. She'd have to find a way to avoid letting her talk about any dates the two of them have or she might have to find another publisher.

"How long have you been published? I'm assuming at least a little while. The last book Alyssa had in her office was number…eight, I think."

"It was seven. Number eight of that series comes out next month. And about four years now as a writer, I guess. My first book came out the spring I turned twenty. I have about twenty-eight out right now." His low whistle made her blush. "It's not all that hard. I have a lot of them finished yet to be given to her."

His laughter made her look around the busy restaurant. She didn't like attention centered on her and this was much more than she could handle. Gathering up her things she started to tell him that she was going to go. So when he stood too, she assumed he was finally going as well.

But he followed her to her car. When he took the keys from her and opened her door she looked up at him. It was then that she could see the humor on his face. She thought if he was going to make fun of her she'd rather he do it here than inside. "Look, why don't you go home? I'll make sure I get Chastity's number, but I'll need to—"

His mouth covered hers. Heat and need slammed into her. Before she could really begin to enjoy him, he pulled away. He leaned his forehead onto hers and held her with just his hand gripped tightly on her arm. "I don't want her number." He kissed her briefly again. "Get in the car, Jasmine. Right now before I get us both arrested right here."

"Arrested?" She moaned when he rocked into her. His cock was hard and she almost begged him to fuck the police and take her please, right now.

She fumbled with the door until he handed her her keys and opened the door for her. She was trembling so hard she couldn't make the key slide into the ignition once she got inside. She knew she couldn't drive. Hell, she could barely breathe. When the passenger door opened and he got inside she dropped the keys on the floor when he pulled her to him.

~~~

Nathan pulled her over the seat toward him, thankful for the bench seat. Her fingers wrapped in his hair even as he shifted in the seat to pull her to him and took her mouth again. Settling her across his lap Nathan cupped her ass and brought her to his groin as his tongue slid along hers. Nathan felt her moan as her breasts pressed against his chest and his fingers dug into her ass.

He only wanted a taste. A quick taste of her and he'd take her home. Lifting her blouse up he buried his face between her breasts. Warm and soft, he lifted them up and laved his tongue over the tops of her bra. When her fingers tightened more in his hair, he slid his thumb up under the cup and brushed it over her pert nipple. Her thighs gripped his hips and she rocked over him.

"Baby. Open your bra. I want to suckle at your nipples, please?" She jerked at the tiny clasp and spilled her full breasts into his palms. "Christ, they're beautiful." Nathan took the pink tip into his mouth and nipped. Her desperate moaning of his name had him open his mouth over her flesh and take as much into his mouth as he could. Even that wasn't enough. He had to have her. Right now. He was trying to roll her to her back on the seat when a loud horn startled them both.

A car right next to them was only about a foot from them. The passengers were getting inside and someone apparently hit the horn. None of the people looked over at them. Had they, there probably would have been a great deal more than horns blaring.

Nathan slowly pulled her blouse down so as not to draw undue attention to them. Her face was buried into his shoulder and he could feel her heavy breathing down his neck. When the car pulled away Nathan sat Jazzie on the seat next to him.

"Are you all right?" She nodded. "Jasmine, look at me. Please?" She continued to look down and not speak. Finally, he lifted her chin up and made her look at him.

"I want to go home. Please. I just…I want to go home."

"All right," he told her gently. "But we need to talk about this. We need to…this isn't what I meant to happen."

Chapter 4

Ginny looked over the report she'd just gotten. It had a great deal of useless information in it and even what she could use was not what she wanted. She knew most of it, like the fact that Jasmine lived alone. That she had no job and that she was pretty much a waste of human flesh.

There were things in it like she owned a twenty-year-old car that burned oil, her dry cleaner said she owned one dress that was worn to shine in places, and her shoes were also in ill repair. She had no bank account that they could find and most of the time she ate at fast food restaurants.

She was either poorer than she and Guinevere were, or she was keeping her money under her mattress and she didn't spend a dime on anything. Ginny thought she didn't have a dime to spend and, because of it or in spite of it, she used everything until it was dust. The girl didn't even live off her brother's money, but worked enough to pay her rent to some broad named Blackwell.

Ginny saw Guinevere out of the corner of her eye. She'd been not speaking to her for days, but needed her right now. So instead of saying she was sorry, though Ginny still didn't believe she'd done anything wrong, she simply launched into what she'd gotten from the cheap PI.

"Your daughter, the middle one, sure doesn't make it easy for us to get her. The girl doesn't do anything but once before moving on to something else." They'd given up on trying to kill the men and decided to simply kill the children. They were much stronger than the girls were and they didn't react the way they'd hoped. Stupid pricks.

"Jasmine Zinnia has always been the stupid one. I doubt anyone would miss her if we were to right-out kill her." Guinevere moved around and Ginny wanted to yell at her to stop, but she spoke before she could. "Lilliane Iris still won't talk to me and now Cain is mad at me. I don't know what she has to be mad about. I was only trying to help."

Ginny had told Guinevere to keep her mouth shut at the very least a dozen times about Lilliane marrying the cop. *Just let it go*, she'd told her. *Don't bring attention to yourself.* But had she listened? No, and now look. Even if they were to get Lilliane now, everyone would suspect her and then they would find Ginny. Not something she was willing and ready for people to know.

"I'd be pissed at you too if you used my middle name with my first all the time. And what the hell were you thinking naming them after flowers? Did you hope they'd be pretty as a garden or some shit like that?" Ginny laughed when Guinevere flushed. "You did, didn't you? Well, they aren't. They're like a cancer on my and your lives. The sooner we rid the world of them, the better."

"What are your plans with Jasmine Zin…Jasmine? I think I'd like to be more helpful with her. She should have been the first one we got rid of. Then worked our way up from there. She'll be easy, I think."

Ginny thought so too, but then she'd figured the teacher would be as well. Who would have thought that a stupid school teacher would have caused them so much trouble? When she'd hired those idiots to kill her Ginny wished she'd had them blow up the school and not mess with taking just one teacher out.

"I have a plan, but it's sort of complicated. I want to make sure that we can get this one done before we move. I've already hired two men to do the deed, but they can't act until we get the little twit alone." A thought occurred to Ginny. "I don't suppose you want to handle that part, would you? Maybe invite her out to lunch and see where we get with that."

Guinevere was nodding before Ginny finished asking. "Yes, I can do that. I can tell her we should have lunch sometime and then when you're ready, I can call her. Yes, I like that plan."

Ginny waited until Guinevere went away before she made notes in the note pad. She really didn't think that Guinevere would go for it and was wondering how she could make it happen on her own. Jazzie was much too gullible for her tastes, but she thought maybe her mother was right. Taking out this child might be a piece of cake. Ginny made another notation before she got up and hid the books away. There was no reason to believe that Guinevere would get cold feet and turn her in, but one did not take a chance with the insane. Ginny was just laying down when she felt Guinevere coming back. She was surprised by that. They only talked when they could see each other.

"I forgot something. I have an appointment with Cain tomorrow. I have to be at his office at eleven-thirty to talk to him."

Ginny acknowledged her, but didn't speak. It was hard like this when they spoke and sometimes it wore her out. More and more, as a matter of fact, she felt...well, drained. Ginny decided to speak to Cain about it the next time she saw him. She closed her eyes as she smiled. She could not wait to get a piece of that man.

Something woke her. Ginny wasn't sure what it was because normally Guinevere woke when there was something going on and called her if she needed her. Ginny lay very still. The not knowing made her very uncomfortable.

She got up quietly, not wanting to alert whoever was inside the house, if indeed someone was, nor did she want to take any chances that she could be hurt. Ginny made her way to the kitchen, where she saw a light coming from under the door. Picking up the large vase that sat near the doorway Ginny went into the room quickly.

Nothing. No one was there and she could see nothing out of order. She looked at the kitchen door, the one that led out to the garage, and found it unlocked. The glass panel was shattered. When she stepped forward she cut herself on a piece of the glass and it made her cry out.

"What happened?" Guinevere said as she appeared. "Oh my, you've cut yourself. Wrap it up, quickly. Do you want us to get infected?"

Ginny simply ignored her. *Really,* she thought to herself, *wrap it up?* Fucking moron. She took a deep breath before she spoke. "I'm aware of the consequences if it gets dirty, Guinevere. And why didn't you wake up when someone broke in? Do I have to fucking do everything?"

"I didn't hear anything." Ginny wrapped her foot as Guinevere continued. "I swear to you, I didn't hear anything. Did they take anything?"

"How the hell should I know? I've been taking care of my fucking foot." The blood soaked through the towel even as she continued wrapping it. "It's going to need stitches. Now what the fuck do we do?"

Guinevere, in her usual non helpful manner, didn't answer. Ginny reached for another towel and wrapped it around her foot again. She was going to bleed to death at this rate. When she started to talk to Guinevere again, she realized she was gone. That's when she saw it.

There had been no reason to look on that end of the counter when she'd walked in. There had been a pile of junk there since they'd moved in. Some of it was hers and the rest, most of it anyway, belonged to Guinevere. They had been saying they were going to sort through it for months.

But she felt one of them would have noticed the blood. It was fresh too, bright red instead of the rust color that it became after it sat for a while. Ginny traced the blood path from the pile of paper all the way up the side of the refrigerator to the top. She clamped her hand over her mouth before she let out a scream.

The neighbor had a dozen cats. Most of them were kittens, of course. The mother cat had dropped about eight or so of them several weeks ago. There had been a couple of other large cats, but other than noticing the pregnant one, Ginny had never paid any real attention to the stupid things. The tom, an orange-and-gray-colored cat, had been hanging around for what Ginny had thought was another piece of ass.

Right now, the tom was sitting atop her refrigerator with his throat slit and his eyes wide open. Standing up Ginny hobbled a bit closer to see that he had been eviscerated as well. His guts lay out to drip over the top and his blood stained boxes of cereal that had been stored there. That's when she saw the little card.

"Stay away from the Waite Family or else this could be you."

Ginny stumbled back to the chair and nearly missed it when she tried to sit. Someone knew. Someone knew. Someone knew. Someone knew, her mind kept repeating over and over. With trembling hands she picked up the stack of towels lying on the table that she'd gotten out to wrap her foot and began to unfold and refold them. She did this four times before she pushed them away. She never let her mind think about what this meant, simply did the chore until she could think past the note. But that hadn't worked out for her. Not yet at any rate.

Calling for Guinevere would be a waste of time. Not only that, but she'd be hysterical and that would do no good other than to piss Ginny off. Right now she'd like to hit someone, but hitting Guinevere wouldn't serve the purpose.

Someone knew. Or, at the very least, thought they knew. That wasn't as bad, but it could be. She wondered if it could be Guinevere, but dismissed that. Ginny would know if it were her and then there was the simple fact that Guinevere could barely cut up a chicken for dinner much less try and cut up a big tom cat. No, she was much too squeamish.

The money-grubbing whore came to mind next. But again, this wasn't her style. Ginny knew she'd have called the cops in...hell, she might even have called in the Feds for all she knew, and then it would be all over. No, she was much too rich to get her hands dirty. Ginny didn't think she'd even have someone do it. Again, she was a mostly by the book sort of bitch and wouldn't do this.

She mentally marked off the cops too. The first one might have the stomach for it, but he would have waited around to see her reaction. And the other one would have signed his name to the card just to piss her off. No, it wasn't one of the family members. It had to be someone who thought they might know, but didn't have enough to go to the cops—not yet at any rate. But who?

Ginny found some tape in the laundry room and taped the stack of towels over the hole. She didn't clean up the glass. She figured she'd been cut; Guinevere could clean up the mess. She was going back to the bedroom, leaving a trail of blood behind her, when she remembered the cat.

Fuck it. Again, she'd been cut. Guinevere was very capable of handling one dead cat. Besides, since she wanted to become more involved in killing off her kids, she'd have to get used to a little blood. Because, for the next kid, she was going to make sure there were buckets of blood.

~~~

Nathan wanted to stay and finish talking with Jasmine. Well, he actually wanted to stay and finish what they'd started in the car, but he'd been called back to the office by his sister. She had told him to take his time, but after all she'd done for him he couldn't do that. Jasmine had gone on to her home and he'd gone to work. But she had asked him to keep quiet about what he'd discovered.

Now here it was, three in the morning and he was wide awake. Wide awake and horny as hell. He glanced down at the three books he'd picked up at the bookstore on his way home from work. That was the reason he was standing in his kitchen with a stone hard erection and no way to relieve himself.

Christ, who knew that Jasmine Waite could write that sort of thing? It wasn't just the sex, though Christ love a duck, that was more than he'd expected. But the story had been amazing. Both of them, as a matter of fact. The way she'd written the characters and the plot made him want to go out and get the rest of them to see if they were nearly as good.

He knew too that she was more than likely writing from her own life. He'd heard stories about the Waite family. You couldn't live in this area for very long and not have heard about how Roscoe Waite and his wife had treated their children. Or not heard how the fucking ass had taken Quinn as a hostage and put a gun to her head demanding that Alyssa pay what was owed him. The man had gotten it in his head that he was owed the reward for finding Alyssa.

His sister had been missing for nearly ten years when Roscoe had done this. Nathan's mother and Alyssa's had tried to have his sister declared dead to get to the money that had been left to her by her father. But someone would send in a picture of Alyssa and the papers would have a heyday

35

about how she'd been found. Of course, it was Cain who had actually found her.

He'd been in the hospital waiting on his mother's surgery to be over when Alyssa had walked in. She'd been there to get some medicine for one of the homeless people she'd been living with all that time. Another man, Moon, had cut her badly and she had also been hoping to get medical treatment. But she'd passed out before she could get away and Cain had treated her. And that, he thought with a smile, was just the beginning for the two of them.

Nathan picked up the book again and opened it at random. His cock surged when he started to read an excerpt. He wondered if at anytime she'd ever done the things she wrote about.

"Suck on my cock, love. I want, no, I need to come down your luscious throat and fill you with my cum." He tangled his fingers in her hair and guided her to take him. "That's it, baby. Oh Christ, your mouth is so hot."

Matthew pumped hard and deep, his cock touching the back of her throat even as she gripped his shaft in her small hand. When she reached beneath his cock for his balls and began to roll them he felt them tighten and fill. But he didn't want to come just yet and knew that if he didn't slow this down he wouldn't last until he tasted her. Pulling his cock free of her mouth with a small pop he reached down and lifted her up.

He devoured her. Her mouth was swollen from his cock and he nipped at her lower lip as he walked her back toward the chair. Matthew wanted to taste her pussy, spear her with his tongue, and drink from her.

"Sit down. Put your ass at the end so that I can fuck you with my mouth, Lidia." Her moan nearly undid him. "Hurry or I'll be forced to punish you again. You remember what I did before, don't you?"

She looked ready to refuse. He knew she remembered what he'd done to her and she wanted it again. Before she refused him and forced his hand again he turned her and pushed her into the chair. He dropped before her, pulled her bare ass to the very edge of the chair and entered her deep with his fingers.

"You can't come until I say so. You do and I won't let you play next time. I'll tie you to the bench and torture you until you beg me to give you release. Understand?"

Her juices ran down his hand and to his elbow. He stopped fucking her and held her still until she looked up at him. He waited, knowing that she knew what he wanted.

"Yes. I won't come. Not until you beg me to." Her grin made his cock ache. He needed to dominate her, but there were times like now that he wanted her sass, wanted her to disobey so that he could do what he—

Nathan tossed the book across the room. He hurt and that was not helping. He opened his pants and freed his cock. He began to stroke it as he imagined Jasmine. He knew that if he didn't get some relief he'd be hurting tomorrow. Hell, he was hurting right now so badly that he wanted to go to Jasmine's house and demand that she let him do all the things that Matthew and Lidia had done to each other.

His phone ringing had him tightening his grip on his cock. He looked over at the caller ID. He frowned when he saw Jasmine's name there. He picked up his phone with his free hand and continued to torment himself. He couldn't imagine what she wanted.

"Are you injured? Something wrong?" he asked in way of greeting. She didn't answer him right away "Jasmine? Please answer me."

"Can you come here? Now? Please?" He nearly swallowed his tongue. Before he could ask her why, what she needed, she continued. "I want you. I…about today, we didn't finish and I want you to. I can't sleep."

He stood up and adjusted his cock. He pinched his phone at his shoulder as he zipped his pants up, nearly catching himself in the teeth. He hissed between his teeth as he reached for his keys.

"I can be there in...do you have protection? I don't...I've not had to use anything in a long time and I don't have anything here."

"Yes. I have condoms. Is that all right?" He nearly leapt for joy. "I have cream as well. I got them today before...after I left the restaurant."

Nathan leaned over and laid his head on the table before he passed out. The sudden rush of blood leaving his head and going lower made him think he wasn't going to make it. He spoke to her from his position. "Jasmine, I've been reading your books. The ones that... Christ, woman, I want you to do those things to me. *I* want to do all those things to you as well." He heard her giggle. "Are you trying to kill me?"

"No. I was just thinking about phone sex. Have you ever done it? I haven't." He sat in the chair knowing now that he wasn't going to be able to stand when she lowered her voice. "Have you ever imagined what someone was doing and had them describe it to you?"

He reached over, turned off the kitchen light, and freed his cock again. He leaned back in his chair as he told her what he was going to do to her. "No, but I've been sitting here wondering if your pussy tasted as good as your mouth. I was thinking that I'd like to take that pert nipple into my mouth again and suckle it as you rode me." Her moan made him bolder. "I want to feel your pussy tighten around my cock as you come. Then I want to roll you to your knees and fuck you hard from behind while I watch your breasts bounce back and forth for me."

"Nathan," she moaned his name. "Please, I want to come. I've changed my mind. Come here and help me."

A stream of pre-cum ran down along his cock and he used it to make his slide smoother. "I can't, baby. I'm in no condition to drive. My cock is so hard I'd never be able to put it back in my pants. Tell me what you're doing right now and, if you make me come, I'll come over there and eat you."

"I have my fingers in my pussy. Three of them are working me hard. I keep thinking about your cock and feeling it against my pussy today and I wonder how it will feel to have you deep inside of me. Would you like that?"

"Yes," he hissed. He slowed down, wanting to make this last while wanting to hurry so he could get to her.

"But now that you've mentioned eating me it's all I can think about. Your head between my legs, your mouth on my clit. Oh, Nathan, my clit is so hard and every time I brush my finger over it I want to scream out my release."

"Don't come, baby. I want to drink your climax from you." His balls tightened as he thought of her pretty clit. "I'm close, baby. Put me over the edge so I can come to you and fuck you."

"Nathan," she screamed.

His cock exploded as she yelled out his name again. When she whimpered and moaned he felt his cock surge again; cum splashed on his chest and groin as he fisted himself. He'd never had a climax feel so painful and so good at the same time. As he continued to pull at his cock he imagined her on the bed drained and sated for now.

He waited for her to speak as he reached for a napkin. He could barely move, but also knew that he wanted to go to her. When he heard her heavy sigh he grinned, wondering if she'd use this in her next book.

"That was fantastic. Oh God, I've never..." He waited for her to continue. He actually waited for her to tell him that he didn't need to come over now, that she was okay on her own. Her next words made his heart leap. "I do hope that the real thing is as good as this aperitif."

"You still want me to come over?" As soon as he asked he felt stupid. More like a school boy than he had sounded coming in his hand just now. "I'm sorry, that didn't come out right."

"I want things to come out right. I want you to come inside of me while I sit on your cock and ride you. Will you be…recovered enough by the time you get here?"

"Yes," he answered on a strangled moan. "I'm nearly there now."

Her laughter made his cock jerk in his hand. "Then hurry because I'm way ahead of you."

Chapter 5

She went to the door four times to check if she missed his knock. She had a doorbell that worked; the UPS guy used it just today when he'd delivered her books. But she didn't want him to think that she'd changed her mind. She looked in the mirror again as she walked by it.

If this little thing didn't tell him that she was ready for him then nothing would. She turned sideways and looked at the back...the lack of back. She'd done more than shop for condoms when she'd left him at the parking lot. A trip to her favorite shop made her nearly max out her credit card.

The light blue robe hid nothing. There were no sleeves, but two dark blue ribbons that held the see-through gauzy material over her breasts as it draped to the floor. Beneath it was a short nightie that revealed more than it covered. The triangles over her breast were so small that they barely covered her nipples. The lace around the material was also dark blue and tied at her shoulders. It opened in the front all the way to the top of the skimpy panties that had a smaller triangle than those that covered her nipples. Turning around, she could see that the only material there was the robe and ribbon. Once the cover was off, she was completely naked in the back other than the string between her ass cheeks and the ones holding the nightie together. She heard his car crunch on the gravel of her driveway.

Going to the door she really had to refrain from tearing the door open, grabbing him inside, and then throwing him to the floor. The climax that she'd had earlier only seemed to intensify her need for this man. When he knocked she counted to three before opening it. She smiled at her trembling hands and nearly fell over when she saw him.

"I see we had the same idea," he said in a low, sexy voice she'd heard him use on the phone. "I like your outfit. It's going to look very good on the floor when I take it from you."

He had on a pair of low-rider jeans and a leather jacket. Nothing else other than his shoes. She had to swallow three times before she could make her tongue work and then once more when he walked inside and locked the door behind him.

"Nathan, you want to—"

"Oh, yes. I very much want to. With you, several times." He kissed her, deep and hungry. "Where is your bedroom, Jasmine? I can't wait much longer to see you over me."

He scooped her up into his arms when she pointed to the stairs. She wanted to protest about her being too heavy, but they were up the stairs before she could manage a single word. Pointing to the room at the end of the hall, she found herself standing next to the bed in no time, his mouth over hers again.

Jazzie pulled his coat down his shoulders. His skin was warm, almost hot, and he smelled so good. When she buried her face in his neck and nipped at his flesh, she felt his moan as it worked up his chest. She looked up at him when he tilted her chin up with his finger.

"I shaved before I left. I had to take my time so I wouldn't miss any whiskers. I don't want to burn you while I have you." She felt her pussy cream when she thought about where he'd not want to burn her. "I can smell you, your climax, in this room. It smells delicious. And I want to taste it on you."

She reached for his pants, wanting to taste him as well, but he stayed her hand with his own. She looked back up at him. He simply shook his head and told her to lie down. She turned and started to crawl to the middle of the bed when he stopped her again.

His eyes looked hungry. She could see his need reflected there and she moaned. When he lifted the robe up off her ass and palmed her, she rocked back into his heat. She felt the string give as he tore it from her hips. When his finger slid down her ass to her pussy she moaned again and buried her face in the bed.

"I can't wait to feel your pussy wrapped around my cock. Open your legs for me. I'm going to fuck you with my tongue like this." Her body didn't even hesitate as her thighs opened, her knees braced on the mattress. "That's it. Christ, I don't think I've ever seen anything more beautiful."

She felt the bed shift beneath her as he came up behind her. Her juices trickled down her leg and she cried out when she felt his tongue trace it back up to the source. His bare cock slid between her legs and touched her clit. She would have come if he hadn't brought his hand down hard on her ass at the same time. Before she could turn he was jerking her hips back to his cock.

"Don't." She didn't move as he plunged his fingers deep into her pussy without touching her clit. "I told you not to come and you did. You didn't expect me to forget that, did you?"

"Nathan, I—" His hand came down twice more. Her pussy fluttered and she could feel her climax building.

"Nathan what?" She didn't answer him, not sure how to. "I said, Nathan what? You'll have to learn to obey me when we're here, Jasmine. I like to play. I won't hurt you. Ever. But I like it when you do what I tell you." He leaned over her and bit her shoulder hard enough to make her whimper. "Are you going to have a problem with that?"

"No," she said softly. "Are you into bondage?"

He smacked her ass again before he answered. "Yes. That and more. I should have told you before I came over here. But you seemed to... You'll let me play with you, won't you?"

She couldn't answer. Her body was on fire from just her mind trying to think of what the "and more" meant. She nodded then answered him on a choked yes.

"Good. You and I are going to have fun, but as I've said, I'd never hurt you. Do you believe me?" He moved his soaked fingers to her ass again and began to play with her tiny hole. She moaned before she could answer yes. "You'll need a safe word. Do you know what that is?"

"Yes," she answered again. "I did some research on bondage for a book recently. I even got to spend a few hours with a Dom and his sub. He wanted to play with me too, but—" His hand came down harder than ever. Then she felt his mouth over the hot area and his tongue laving her. She moaned again, unable to believe how wonderful it felt.

"Never will you play with someone else. You...you belong to me now until we decide that we want to part. I don't even want you going to another club unless I'm with you." His hand came down again, but this time, he smoothed it with soft cresses. "You belong to me now, Jasmine. Mine."

~~~

Nathan moved over her soft skin. His hands couldn't seem to stop touching her, not that he wanted to. He should have told her, should have asked her if she had ever done this before and would she mind... No, he wouldn't think of that. She'd said yes, she understood. Or she soon would.

44

"There are rules. I establish them and you obey. Understand?" His cock jerked when she said yes. "I am your Master. You'll obey me, slave."

"I…may I ask questions?" He heard the tremor in her voice and it made him want to take her now.

"Yes. Tonight. After this, you'll never question me on what I want from you. Once you understand the way things will be, you'll decide whether or not this is something you want to pursue. Do you understand?"

He found himself wanting her to tell him now that she didn't want this. He knew what he was asking her was something…well, he'd always thought of it as too dark for most people. He was not sure that he wanted her to know this part of him. It was why he'd stayed away from her for all this time. Why he stayed away from most women.

"I know that you said you'd not hurt me, but…well, I don't like pain. Not at all. My father was an abusive man and he would hurt me…he…he…"

He waited for her to finish. He knew that what she said was going to be something she'd never shared before, but he waited. Moving his hand down along her inner thigh he gathered the cream there and moved it to her small rosette. Working the pad of this thumb over and around it he thought about taking her there and his cock hardened more. Just when he thought he was going to punish her again she spoke.

"He raped me." Her voice was small and low. His heart went out to her. "I've…therapy helped, but there are still times when I feel overwhelmed when someone…a man is too close. Sometimes…most of the time, I can't come, I can't climax. And never as powerful as I did over the phone with you."

He leaned down and kissed her back, laved his tongue along her spine as he moved back from her body. Her whimper nearly had him returning, but he needed her to trust

45

him. With a short, "roll over," he positioned her on her back as he untied the ribbons of her gown.

"This isn't about pain; it's about the pleasure. I'm going to withhold things from you, especially your climaxes, so that when I do allow you to come it will be all the more intense for the both of us." He put her hands above her head and showed her without words to keep them there. "If you ever feel the need to stop, you need only tell me to by using your safe word and I'll stop immediately. Have you thought of one?"

"Yes. White-out. I understand that there are colors too? Ones that I use to tell you that you need to slow down?" He nodded, glad she had some understanding of what was going to happen. "I used the traffic lights in my book. I would like to use those as well."

That meant that if she said *green* if he asked her, she was fine, *yellow* to slow it a bit, and *red* to stop only what he was doing and not the play. He opened her legs wide and then crawled back on the bed to sit on his heels between them. Christ, she was soaking wet and she smelled like a banquet to him.

"I want you to keep your pussy bare for me. Starting tomorrow, if possible. When I eat you I want nothing to bar my way. I also want you to wear no panties and skirts when you come to see me. And you will, daily. I want you to come into my office and present yourself to me." He reached down and began to stroke his hard cock. "Do you like to suck cock?"

"I don't...I've never done it before. I actually don't enjoy...I've never really liked sex before this." He looked up at her when she said that. "I always thought it was sort of a messy way to get close to someone."

He'd read her books, particularly the sex, and he thought maybe he knew why sex had not meant that much to her. She was a closet sub and most of her scenes said that. He nodded.

"Tonight is about rules. Then we'll go over what I want from you as we progress. Are you still with me, Jasmine?"

She nodded then spoke again. "Do you have toys, Nathan? Things that you'll use on me? Things that you'll strap me to?"

"No, not really. I've never found...I've been looking for a sub first. I've been... I'll be honest with you, Jasmine. I've spent most of my life, even as a child, either drunk or high on one form of drugs or another. And before you ask, I'm clean. It seems that a drunk or addict can't really have sex well. Probably because we can't have a good erection and, when we do, it's usually short lived."

"Then how did you, I mean, how did you know this is the kind of sex you wanted?" Such an innocent question, one she had a right to ask.

"Because, like you, I was raped. Not by my parents, but by some of the people who were supposed to treat me. I found that I liked it. And as I got older, stronger, it was then that I realized I could tie them down and have my way. I got a bigger satisfaction than when they tied me down."

She didn't say anything. He waited and watched her face to see if she was sickened by his admission. She only nodded at him. Nathan felt his breath whoosh from his lungs at her acceptance. He'd never told anyone that before, not even his own therapist.

Nathan wanted to reward her and he knew just what to do. He leaned down to her center and inhaled her scent. Heavenly. He spread her thighs open and watched as her nether lips fluttered. He couldn't wait to taste her and ran his tongue deep into her cleft.

"I want you to come as much as you want while I eat you. I want to taste this creaminess and lick it from you. Understand me?" She nodded. He pinched her thigh. "You'll answer me when I ask you something or I may change my mind."

"Yes. I understand." She tilted her hips up to his mouth. "Please. I beg you."

He licked her again, ignoring her clit and not giving her the climax they both wanted. "You'll clarify what I tell you so that I won't have to punish you unnecessarily. And you'll never beg me. You will also call me 'Master' when you speak to me in the bedroom or when we are at play. And you will be simply 'slave.' Understand?"

"I will call you 'Master' and I will be your slave. I don't beg and I'll..." He heard the catch in her voice and knew that she was enjoying this. "I'll clarify what you tell me so that you won't have to punish me."

"Good slave." He suckled her clit into his mouth; at the same time, he buried two of his fingers deep into her channel. Her scream of release tore from her throat. He didn't stop as she flooded his hand, but continued to drink her juices as she rode his mouth.

Nathan couldn't believe how responsive she was. Even when he moved his wet fingers to her ass she moaned. Using his small finger he plunged inside of her as he fucked her with his tongue. She came six times quick and hard before he sat up and fisted his cock. When he asked her for a condom she pointed to the small table next to the bed and he grabbed one and handed it to her.

"Sheath me, slave. Then roll to your back. I'm going to fuck you hard." She dropped the wrapper twice before she got it open. Then she was trembling so hard she had some difficulty rolling it over him. Nathan nearly came twice with her fingers touching him so intimately.

When she rolled to her knees he was deep inside of her before she was completely ready for him. He grabbed her hips and held her tight as he pistoned inside of her. He was so close that he knew that if she tightened around him again

48

like she had his fingers and tongue he was going to explode. Leaning down over her, pressing her into the mattress, he bit her shoulder and felt her come apart. Nathan's vision blurred as he came. His entire body convulsed hard over and over as he jettisoned deep inside of her rippling channel. Then he simply dropped on her and rolled at the last second, taking her with him. He was tumbling into sleep when he heard her moan again. Nathan smiled. He'd found his sub.

Chapter 6

Alyssa watched her brother. There was something different about him today. She'd been trying to remember if it was a haircut, or maybe he'd gotten a new suit, but he was walking around the office as if he had springs on his feet. She smiled when he seemed to stop in mid-step and smile before moving on. Whatever had put that bounce in his step and the odd smile on his face, she was happy for it.

"Mrs. Waite, there's a call for you on line two. It's Mr. Jacobson from the Atlanta office. He wants you to tell him what the numbers mean for the account down there. He seems to think there has been a breach of some sort."

Alyssa looked at her assistant, Mable. "Did he say which account?" She nodded and handed her a note. Alyssa brought the account up on her computer before she opened the line. She scribbled a small note telling Mable to get her brother and Drew. "Mr. Jacobson, it's Alyssa. How's it going besides this number issue?" She couldn't see anything, but continued to look. Sometimes it was just an accounting error of only a few pennies that had her accountant calling her and asking her to clear something up. She went down the long column of numbers to see if she could recall anything that might have changed.

"It's fine, Mrs. Waite. I just…I know how you don't like mistakes on the money that goes out so I keep a close eye on it for you. But this is a little more...well, Mrs. Waite, I was really surprised by this one."

Her office door opened and both her brother and Drew walked in. She smiled when she saw that even with a call to the office Nathan still looked happy. She put the phone on speaker and told Mr. Jacobson who was in the room with her.

"What accounts are we supposed to be looking at, Tim?" Nathan asked. "Maybe that'll narrow down what we're looking at."

"It's that project that you are working on, Mr. Howard, the Madison Avenue project. There is a large...well, a very large sum of money going out that I have no receipt for. And I've looked several times for it. You're usually so very good at giving me all those at the end of the week both in email and in the courier package that I get. I've looked—"

Alyssa knew that if he was allowed the man would over explain everything. She was glad when Drew cut him off early this time. He would give her a headache in no time.

"Give me the date. I have it pulled up on my laptop along with Alyssa's computer. And if you have a sum, that'll help as well." Drew reached into her small refrigerator and took them all out a bottle of water before he continued. "Also, do me a favor and close your door, please. We don't need everyone knowing what we're doing."

Alyssa smiled. She knew that the man was hopping up to do so. He seldom remembered to eat much less close his door when talking to her. It wasn't as though she was worried about being overheard, but she knew that she, as well as Drew, seldom watched their language when they were into something.

Nathan pulled his chair around to her side of the desk and they watched as the files flew by. When they'd gotten to the correct entry she frowned. A knock at the door had Nathan going to it and coming back with his own laptop. He moved back to where she was sitting and the three of them looked at the different entries.

The one from the accountant, the one on Alyssa's computer, said there was a debit of eight thousand four hundred twenty-three dollars and twelve cents paid out to TMP, or The Madison Project. On both Drew's and Nathan's it said twenty-three dollars and thirteen cents. A difference of eight thousand four hundred dollars.

"I didn't take that," Nathan said quickly. "I wouldn't cheat you, you have to believe me."

"Of course you didn't. What a stupid thing to say. Mr. Jacobson, we have a slightly different amount at this end. Do you have a receipt for twenty-three dollars and some change?" She clicked at the top of the column that listed where the debits were going to and put the list in alphabetical order rather than date. She watched as both Drew and Nathan did the same.

"Oh yes, ma'am, I do. It is marked with Mr. Howard's initials just as he always does. But...well, Mrs. Waite, the money is missing as well. The difference, you see. If it were a mistake that way, we'd have the monies, but someone took the entire amount."

Alyssa moved back from her desk to let Nathan have access to her computer. He was making notations on hers by highlighting several different entries while Drew was clicking on them and reading the receipts.

When they'd started out with his project Nathan had suggested that they scan each receipt and attach it to the entry. That way they would be able to see just what they'd purchased or paid with a simple click without having to dig through boxes and files of them. It had worked out well. And now it was helping them in ways she was sure her brother had thought of as well.

"Mr. Jacobson, let me call you back. Don't do anything just yet until you hear from me. I'm sure you know that we're looking into this." She nodded at Drew to disconnect the call when Tim said he'd be waiting for her. "You know that he won't leave his desk until I get back to him, right?"

Drew laughed. "Yes. And if I know him he's right now staring at it willing it to ring back." Drew leaned back in his chair. "This isn't good, Alyssa. So far Nathan has found seven errors—"

"I swear to you I didn't do this," Nathan said with slight panic in his voice. "I wouldn't bite the hand that feeds me and I certainly wouldn't steal from my own family. Alyssa, you have to—"

"That's enough," she said to him gently. "It never occurred to me that you did this. And I knew that you were keeping a good accounting; that's why I asked you in here. Had I thought you were stealing from me I would have simply had Drew come in. Now, let's see what we have."

They worked on it for nearly three hours. They found more than two dozen mistakes. Not all of them large, but the totals were staggering. Nearly four hundred thousand over the past six months.

"I can put a freeze on the account and that way nothing else can go out until you sign off on it," Drew said as he put down his fork. They'd ordered in when it looked like they were going to be here for a while. "It'll stop money from going out without verification, but it still doesn't tell us who it taking it."

"Do you think it's someone in the office in Atlanta or up here? I'd hate to think it was someone who worked with Tim. He takes great pride in the fact that he has the best team in the company." Nathan tossed his own fork into his now empty plate. "I think we need to call in someone who knows a bit about computers to see where the money is being taken from."

Alyssa looked up from her egg roll. "We can do that? Find the person from a computer expert? How, and do you know anyone?"

She knew her brother knew a great many people with less than pristine backgrounds. She'd been surprised and a little overwhelmed by the information he had. First, by what he knew, and secondly, by who he'd gotten if from. It seemed to her that the places he'd been had been little more than places for the very wealthy to get together and teach each other how to become richer.

"Sure. The addresses from where the changes were made should be easy enough to follow. We just have to hunt that down and see where it's located. We can tell if it's in-house or if someone has hacked our system." She must have looked confused because he continued. "The address of the computer is the Internet protocol address or *IP*. Each computer has a specific one attached to it. And each time someone makes an entry or, in this case theft, they are essentially leaving their fingerprints for us to find. I know this guy…well, a couple of them, and I'll give them a call. See what they can find before we do something like piss off the person at the other end."

Alyssa agreed to let them come in and see what they could do. She didn't even tell Nathan to be careful. She knew that he would. Drew called Atlanta back and told him that they were going to be a couple more days before they could give him an answer on the money. Then they told him to not say anything to anyone, especially his staff.

"You don't believe it's one of mine, do you, Mr. Miller? I have worked with these individuals for years and I would trust them with my life."

"It's not your life we're concerned with right now, Tim. It's Mrs. Waite's money. Just keep this to yourself and act as normal as you can. We've got someone working on it from this end and I promise you that we'll keep you informed."

They left her office an hour later. Nathan had called in his expert and Drew asked to do a background check. Nathan agreed, but told Drew not to be surprised by what he found. The name was enough to make her rather uptight lawyer burst out laughing.

"Really? He's a computer hack?" Drew asked Nathan on their way out the door. "I would have thought with his family's money he wouldn't need to cheat the system."

"Well, when your family cuts you off and you feel as if they owe you...well, Daniel thought it was partly their fault for him being a drug addict anyway so he simply helped himself to whatever he wanted when he wanted it. Unlike me. My mother was more than willing to keep me high. When I got out she simply hooked me up with another drug dealer and went about her happy little way."

The door closed behind them before she could say anything. She knew that her mother had been a horrible person, but to enable your own child...well, that really shouldn't have surprised her either. She had drugged her so that her uncle could have sex with her to get her pregnant. Alyssa shuddered. She was so glad that she'd found out before that had occurred.

She picked up her phone to call her knight in shining armor. Her husband Cain was the greatest thing that had ever happened to her next to their son. She smiled when she thought of the news she had for her doctor husband.

"I'm sorry Alyssa, but he's with a patient right now," his nurse Sandy told her. Then she lowered her voice. "It's his mother. She cut her foot really badly and he's had to stitch it up for her."

"Oh my, I bet he's having a blast with that one, isn't he? Did she say how she cut it? Not that I care really, but was just wondering."

Sandy laughed. "You got that. And not that I'm aware of. She just came in yelling for him. Even with the area numbed she's screaming like he's cutting her foot off. I swear I don't know how she could have birthed such a wonderful man and her being…well, her I guess."

Alyssa was still laughing when she hung up a few minutes later. Sandy said she'd have him call her and that she'd make sure that she told him in front of Guinevere. The entire staff had been witness to the fights and screaming matches that she and Guinevere had. The two of them couldn't be in the same room without taking a bite or two out of each other. Alyssa hated the woman and she, in turn, hated Alyssa.

~~~

Jazzie was running behind. Not just a little either, but nearly three hours. The lawyer had made an appointment for ten and hadn't taken her into his office until nearly noon. Then he proceeded to answer the phone when it rang and eat his lunch, which she wanted. She was starving and pissed. Plus, she'd had to go to the grocery twice because she'd forgotten something and had to turn around and get it.

The phone was ringing when she walked in with the last bag of food. She groaned when she saw who it was. She did not want to speak to her mother right now. She tried to smile before picking up the receiver and only succeeded in grimacing.

"I want you to come over here. I hurt my foot and I need you to wait on me. And bring me something for dinner. I'm sick of eating out."

Jazzie pulled the phone from her ear and stared at it before answering her mother. "No. I have plans." Then she felt slightly bad and asked her what she'd done. Since the entire family knew what had happened between their mother and Lilliane on her wedding day Jazzie had decided that she was no longer going to cater to Guinevere. No one said that sort of thing to her sister and got away with it.

"I cut my foot and your brother had to stitch me up. I believe he said he used over a hundred stitches."

Jazzie pulled out her cell phone and sent a question to her brother by text.

Treat M today?

Yes. Cut. 4 stitches. Don't help her. She is k.

"Cain said you were all right and that he used four stitches. And I have plans already. You want someone to help you, apologize to Lilliane and mean it and I'll find someone to come there."

"I will not apologize to your sister. I did nothing wrong but tell her the truth. I can't help it if she's too stupid to realize that she is making a mistake marrying that gimp."

Jazzie hung up before she said something she might not ever regret. She had about an hour before Nathan came over. An hour to do all the things he'd asked her to and some of the things she wanted to do for herself. She was suddenly glad she'd made an appointment with a place she could get herself shaven before she'd gone to the lawyers.

Shifting her hips she smiled at the way she felt. She'd had a trim job before, but not anything like she'd had done today. Nathan had told her completely bare and she hadn't realized that she'd have to get her bottom cleaned as well.

He'd left her early this morning. She'd wanted to stay in bed all day with him, but he'd told her that work had to come before play. He'd given her instructions on what to do and she didn't know what he'd do when he found out she'd not been able to get most of it done. Not even the trip to the local sex shop.

She wondered if his form of punishment was going to be as delicious as last night's. She'd slipped up when she'd come and called him Nathan. He'd bent her over his knee and paddled her ass good with his hands. Then, when she'd cried, he denied her a climax. Smiling she wondered if he knew how much she enjoyed fighting off what she knew was going to be a killer and realized that he more than likely knew.

She was putting the last touches on dinner when she heard him pull into her drive. Going to the front hall she looked out the window and was suddenly glad she'd not stripped down like she'd nearly done. Her sister probably wouldn't have appreciated being met at the door naked.

She opened the door with a smile. "You can't stay. I'm having company and I don't want you here to mess up my plans," she told Sin. "Besides, I thought you were going on some sort of stake out or something."

"No, the guy confessed and there wasn't any…is that roasted chicken I smell? You have to feed me. Payton is on some kind of daddy mission with Emma and I'm starved."

"I said no. I have someone coming over. Now get. I swear if you leave right now I'll make you two chickens and you can eat them all yourself." Sin looked at her oddly. "Please?"

"I'm not leaving until you tell me who it is. You know, I don't believe I've seen you this… It's a man, isn't it? I knew it. I told Quinny you were seeing someone and she swears you aren't. Damn it, I should have—"

They both turned to see the car pulling in beside Sin's vehicle. Sin turned back to look at Jazzie when Nathan got out of the car. She looked shocked and amazed.

"You're seeing Nathan Howard? Well, fuck me! How long?" Sin whispered. "Fuck, this is great. I like him."

"Hush. And if you tell anyone I'll tell Payton where your big stash is. And you know how he feels about you eating healthy." Nathan stepped up on the porch when Sin started to speak.

"Hello, Sydney. I thought you were on a stake out or something. Did something happen?" Jazzie was surprised when Nathan pulled her to him and kissed her quickly on the mouth. "I guess you were on your way out?"

Sin laughed. "Yes, but not by choice. I didn't know you two were seeing each other. Or are you keeping it a secret?"

"Sin, please. This is... We're just... Damn it, Sin, why did you have to come by now?"

"Because if I'd come by later I would have interrupted something. This is good now. Tell me, have you been sleeping together long?"

Nathan laughed when she simply wanted to crawl under a rock. But before she could answer her sister or kill her Nathan answered.

"Not long. And in actuality we haven't done a whole lot of sleeping. But you know how it is. We've only just figured out that we like to screw each other's brains out and, hell, why not?"

Sin waited about two seconds before she burst out laughing. "I guess so. Okay. I'm going now and I'll keep your little secret. For now. But if you don't let me be there when you tell everyone I'm going to be really pissed off." With a quick kiss on Jazzie's cheek, Sin went to her car only to stop halfway there. "Oh, by the way, you should know that when you go to the Body Shoppe to get a trim job you should really park your car around back or take a cab. That's the real reason I'm here."

Chapter 7

"Let me guess, she's not coming?" Guinevere looked in the mirror at the person just behind her as she spoke. "You fucked it up like you did everything else, didn't you?"

Guinevere was afraid of Ginny. Not just a little either. She was violent and sometimes she kept things from her. Like the bloodied cat in the kitchen. She knew she knew something about it, but so far Guinevere hadn't been able to figure it out.

"No," Ginny said sourly. "She's not coming. Cain must have told her that our foot wasn't as bad as we'd planned to tell her. She knew just how many stitches he'd put in your foot."

That was another thing, how had she really cut her foot? She'd told her that she'd walked on some broken glass that had been knocked out of the door. Had she done it to make her feel sorry for her? Guinevere didn't like these games. At least not the ones where she was in the dark and Ginny had all the answers.

"You must have told her. He's not allowed to give out that information because it's something to do with patient-doctor privilege or something. It's against the law for him to share that stuff."

"Not if he thinks it's his mother. Why did you have to go to him anyway? There are several hundred doctors in this area and you had to go to my son?" Guinevere closed her eyes against the pain in her head. "I know you think you can fool anyone about us looking alike, but I've told you Cain isn't the stupid one."

"I had to see him. Christ, do you know what it's like to see that luscious piece of male and not have some of it? Do you have any idea how long it's been since I've had sex?"

Ginny's comments tightened the grip on her already pounding head.

"You can't expect me to wait around here all day long with nothing to do, can you?"

Guinevere cried out when her head felt as if it had a vise around it. It took her a few seconds to realize that her nose was bleeding again. She rushed to the bathroom and pressed a towel to her face as she glared at Ginny's reflection in the mirror. She really was beginning to hate her.

"You should get that looked at. It's a nasty problem you have there." Ginny laughed as she went away.

After cleaning up Guinevere went to the bedroom again and changed. She was becoming more and more convinced that Ginny was keeping things from her. Without thought as to what the other girl thought Guinevere went to Ginny's bedroom and started looking around. Guinevere knew that she only had a few minutes at most before Ginny came back. She was searching under the mattress when she felt something deep under it. She pulled it out when she finally got her fingers around it.

Money. Lots of it, too, if the thick plastic was any indication. She fanned the first stack of hundreds and realized that there was more in this stack than she'd seen in a long while. She put it back in the bag and stuffed it under the mattress. Now that she knew about it she had to figure out why Ginny was hiding it and where the fuck she'd gotten it.

Sitting in the living room she pulled her own stash of things out from under the cushion. There wasn't any money in her baggies, but there were enough drugs there to do what she needed. And what she needed was to put Ginny out for a while. For a long while if Guinevere had any say in the matter. But she knew she couldn't kill her. Not yet at any rate. She still needed her.

Putting her things back under the seat she sat down and propped her feet up. It was horrible of Jazzie to tell her that she wouldn't come over and help. Now she'd have to think of another way to get the girl over here. Guinevere didn't know why, but she felt she was running out of time. She looked around the room and wondered, not for the first time, how she'd gotten in this mess. Her husband was dead and now her kids, all of them, were treating her as if she were the bad guy. That money-grubbing whore Alyssa had caused all this and the sooner she was gone, the better.

All the bitch would have had to have done was pay what was owed. Guinevere would have had her family back the way it was and her Roscoe would be here with her instead of Ginny. He had loved her, she was sure of it, and not Ginny. Ginny.

Ginny had begun sleeping with her Roscoe about a year after *The Incident*. She'd always referred to it like that and not what really happened. She still thought about knowing that Ginny had been there all along, always in the background. And when that had happened, well, there was no going back.

It had been the year that Gracie Anne had left. The girls, all but Gracie Anne, had been at the mall together. She had been ill and had stayed home to take a nap. Guinevere had heard screaming, loud and long, but couldn't move. Couldn't get up off the couch, but lay frozen in place. That was the first time Ginny had been around her children she realized now. And it was the last time that her Roscoe had slept with her.

63

Gracie Anne had claimed that her father, of all people, had raped her and that she, her own mother, had let it happen. No matter how many times she'd tried to explain that she'd known nothing about it Gracie Anne said she'd been there. It had taken three days to get her daughter to return home and then their relationship had never been the same. In fact, every time she came home for a visit Gracie Anne never said a single word to her. A daughter shouldn't treat her mother that way. There should be friendship and...she never got anything from Gracie Anne, she realized. All the other girls did; dresses, coats, even their wedding dresses and other naughty items, but never her own mother. Guinevere frowned. She didn't even call her on her birthday or Mother's Day.

She picked up the phone to call her daughter when she realized that she didn't know the number. What kind of daughter didn't give her mother her number? She started to put the phone back when she realized that it wasn't working. The phone was dead.

Hobbling to the kitchen to see if it was not working there as well she noticed that the blood was still on the floor. She had refused to clean up Ginny's mess last night and she wasn't doing it now. Picking up the phone she found it didn't work either. Their phone had been shut off again.

Damn it, why didn't Cain take care of her? It was his duty to care for his mother, wasn't it? She went back into the living room and sat staring at the television. The cable had been turned off three days ago; that was one of the things she'd mention to Cain when she saw him. She pulled a note pad off the table in front of her and began a list. The next time she saw Cain she was going to be prepared. No more of this fumbling around trying to get him to pay her more money. She wanted him to take care of things.

~~~

Nathan watched Jasmine. She was nervous, he could tell. So was he, if he told the truth. He'd never had a sub of his own before, just the ones he'd been with at the clubs. He watched her move about the kitchen fixing dinner, wondered if she had panties on under her skirt, and he wanted to know what she looked like bare.

The fact that Sin had seen her at the Body Shoppe had been a little bit of a surprise. He knew he'd told her to go, but he expected her to put it off for a few days. His blood heated just thinking about her naked beneath him. Her voice brought him out of his daydreams

"I didn't get to go to the shop today, the one on Tenth. My lawyer was late with our appointment and he kept me longer than necessary. I'm very sorry." She leaned over to get something out of the bottom of the refrigerator and her voice was slightly muffled. "Then my mother called wanting me to drop everything to come and take care of her."

"Who's your lawyer? The reason I'm asking is because I'm assuming you don't use Drew." She nodded as she began to cut the lettuce. He stood up to help her. "I can cut the lettuce if you want. Why not? Why don't you use Drew?"

She handed him the ceramic knife and went back to the stove before she answered. "He would tell Alyssa. No, that's not it. I guess I'm a little embarrassed. I never expected...I never dreamed that anyone would buy my books, and besides, I was already with this other jerk before I even knew Alyssa or Drew."

"I think you should ask him. He'd keep your secret, not that I think you should anymore. But he'd be very quiet about it. He's a good lawyer too. I would use him if I needed legal advice." He put the tomatoes and carrots in the large bowl with the lettuce. Without saying a word she handed him the dressing and he tossed it on the salad.

They were nearly done eating before she said anything more. "I need to make sure...they'll make fun of me. I'm sure of it. I've heard them talk about the author of the books. They think she's some sort of sexy goddess that does nothing but have sex all day and write about it."

His cock jerked to attention. "I could help you with that. It may not be all day, but we could have nothing but sex and you write about it. I thought of that." He lowered his voice as he continued. "The things you write about and wondered if you'd use what I want to do to you in your books."

Need, he could see it in her eyes and in the way she opened her mouth slightly. He could see her breaths; she was panting and her nipples had hardened. When she set her fork and knife down he wondered how he could take her; here on the table or on the counter? But first...

"Come here, slave. Stand before me and show me my pretty pussy." She swallowed twice before she stood up. "Lift your skirt. I want to see if you obeyed me to the letter."

He could see her fingers tremble as she slid her hands down her skirt. He wasn't sure if she was teasing him with how slow she was moving or simply that she was nervous. He didn't touch her. For as much as he wanted to he didn't so much as scoot his chair back. When she had her skirt up over her hips he looked down and nearly whimpered.

She was bare. And she was wet. He could see moisture on her tights and her clit; the tiny little nub he'd had so much fun sucking last night was just peeking out from beneath her lips. He wanted to lean down and take her again, but he also wanted her to suck his cock. Last night she'd told him that's what she'd wanted and now he'd let her.

Nathan moved his chair back as he wiped his mouth with his napkin. He took his time, not because he wanted to make her suffer, but he wanted her so desperately that he thought he might come from just looking at her. He opened his belt and then his pants. She watched him as he reached into his boxers and stroked his cock.

"Tonight you're going to suck me off. And while you do that, you'll not touch yourself unless I tell you. Understand me, slave?"

"Yes. Yes, Master. I will suck your cock and I won't touch myself unless you tell me to." Her voice was deep and full of lust. He watched as a stream of her juices trickled down her thigh.

"Strip." She dropped her skirt and started to undo the buttons on her blouse. "Rip it off you. I want you naked now."

Buttons flew everywhere. He moaned softly when her breasts bounced with the motion. She unsnapped her bra and peeled it down her arms. She was beautiful. When she leaned over and put her fingers into the tops of her stockings his body tightened. The stockings, his favorite kind of thigh-highs, had to stay.

"Leave them on. And I want you to never wear anything but thigh-highs again. When I want to taste you or fuck you I want nothing in my way. Understand?"

"Yes, Master." He could tell she wanted to say more. He could have given her permission to speak, but he was afraid she'd beg him to take her now and he'd do it. This was going to be his way even if it killed him. And it very well might.

"On your knees." When she was down the way he wanted her to be he turned his chair toward her and pulled his pants down around his calves without standing. It wasn't graceful, but he managed to do it. A pearl of pre-cum was on the tip.

He didn't speak. He wasn't sure he could actually, so he rubbed his cock along her lips and she licked him. When she opened her mouth slightly he surged forward deep. It was all he could do not to spill his seed immediately.

"Lick the crown and down along my shaft." He felt her tongue circle his head and he groaned. "That's it. Nip along there. Christ, that's wonderful."

She caught on fast. Soon he was rocking into her sweet mouth as he had her pussy the night before. He could barely manage to remember to breathe; teaching her was out of the question. Besides, if she got any better at this he'd be begging *her* to let him come.

Her hand wrapped around his cock as she licked him like a cone. When their eyes met he knew that she was close to coming herself. She'd done as he'd commanded her to and not touched herself, but she was enjoying herself so much that she didn't need to touch to come. Wrapping his hand in her hair he showed her how he wanted her to take him. He was touching the back of her throat with every surge now. And when she took him deep and swallowed he came.

"Fuck," he shouted as she swallowed him. Every time she tightened around him, he felt his cock pour more down her. Yanking her head off him he lifted her and shoved her over the table. With a sweep of his hand every plate there hit the floor. He was deep inside of her before the last plate broke.

She didn't speak, didn't beg. He wanted her to; he wanted to bring her quickly and hard. He brought his hand down across her ass as he slammed into her. When he reached around her and pinched her clit she screamed out his name and he gathered her cream up and smeared it over her tiny rosette.

"I didn't tell you to make me come, slave. You'll be punished for that now." He slid his thumb into her. She was tight and he doubted she even felt the small pain. "I'm going to stretch this hole for me. I'm going to fuck you here while I fuck you with a dildo. Two cocks deep in you and you can't come."

He worked her ass hard, harder than he knew he should have, but he was beyond thinking and when he felt his balls tighten again he moved another finger in her and heard her scream.

"Color," he demanded of her. "Now, tell me a color."

"Green," she sobbed over and over. "Green, green, green."

He couldn't hold back. He was going to come again. Leaning down to her shoulder he bit her lobe and, with another command for her to come, he spilled his seed deep within her as she shouted out her own release.

Chapter 8

Jazzie was sitting in the lobby of the Howard building the next afternoon. Well, sitting wasn't all she was doing. She was squirming too. She hurt slightly and she was nervous. She thought briefly of why she hurt.

Nathan had made her come so hard last night that she thought she'd pulled some muscles. He'd also stretched her bottom. She smiled when she thought of how sweet he'd been after they'd had sex on the kitchen table. Not only had he run a hot bath for her, but he'd put lotion on her abused muscles and had told her how sorry he was.

She told him she liked that he'd lost control. And his low growl made her wet all over again. He told her that he should have taken his time and that he would from now on, but she was so responsive that he'd just wanted to take her. She wished, in a way, he had. And then he'd made love to her. Slowly and passionately. Her body was on fire for him when he finally took her over the edge. And she only stirred slightly when he'd left her bed.

"Miss Waite, Mr. Miller will see you now," the secretary said, taking her from her musings. Jazzie had a slight moment of panic, but tamped it down as she thanked her and went into his office.

"Jazzie, how the heck are you? Have you come to tell me that you've decided to move in with us and help with the babies?" They both laughed. He'd been asking her that same thing since they'd had the triplets just over a year ago.

She sat down, suddenly unsure if this was a good idea. She started to stand to go when she saw the small note in the top of her bag. Pulling it out, she read the short but very wonderful note from Nathan before putting it deep into her bag.

"I have something to tell you. Something…something you have to swear not to tell another living soul." He leaned forward on his desk as she continued. "I've got a secret. It's not bad. It's just…I don't want anyone to know. Can you do that for me?"

"Yes. You can trust me. Whatever it is, I can help you with it. Or we can work to fix whatever it is you've done. And for the record, it's not always as bad as you think it is."

She laughed. "This is why I didn't think this was such a good idea. I'm not in trouble. And I've not done anything wrong, Drew. I need a lawyer. A good one. Things have taken off in a direction that I now need…I need you." She reached into her bag and pulled out her portfolio. Then the contract. "I got this from my publisher the other day. I'll let you read it and then we'll talk."

He sat back in his chair and opened it. She knew the moment he got to the part where it named her as *Jasmine Blackwell ~ Author*. She watched as he sat up again and started reading it seriously. Jazzie got up, walked to his small refrigerator, pulled out two bottles of water, and put one at his elbow before she opened hers and began walking around the room.

She'd only been in here once before, when her sister Alyssa had asked her about the desk that was no longer in here. She hadn't liked it and neither had Jazzie. Alyssa had told her the desk was too stodgie and she just couldn't imagine anyone feeling very comfortable sitting on either side of it. She'd had it taken away when Jazzie had agreed.

The desk that Drew used now was large and oak. It was solid like the man and warm and comforting like Alyssa had wanted everyone to feel. The rest of the room conveyed the same feelings. Like you could trust the man and the business that was dealt here, a feeling that was important no matter what side of the desk one happened to be on.

The pictures around the room were interspersed with awards. Drew had been a graduate of Harvard Law and had been in the top one percent of his class. There were accolades of his good works too. There were awards for his humanitarian works as well as his help with the homeless shelters that he had helped the Howard Foundation set up. She loved the pictures of him with her family and with his, the ones of his uncle Thomas and of her. She smiled when she saw them all together at Lilliane's wedding just a few months ago.

"Jazzie, how long have you been a famous author?" She came and sat back down at his question. "I'm assuming a while since this mentions a series of books that I know my wife, your sister, has read."

"A while. About ten years, I guess. And famous? I don't know about all that, but I do well." She nodded to the contract. "I fired my lawyer this morning. It wasn't pretty. He can't tell anyone about this, can he?"

"No, not legally he can't. But he may let things slip and then it'll be everywhere. Why?" He opened her portfolio and looked at each cover and the cover wraps she'd had printed.

"I don't know. He was incompetent and he seemed to think I worked for him and not the other way around. Then there was the movie deal. He said that I could do better than what they're offering me.'

"You can. You will. But that's not what I'm talking about and you know it. Why haven't you told your family? You aren't ashamed of what you write, are you? Quinn says they have the greatest sex scenes in them she's ever read."

He flushed before continuing. "I'm sure you're well aware of that."

"Actually, no. When I write a story it's like I'm not really doing it." He looked at her oddly. "I mean, it's me writing it, but I simply let it flow over me like a blanket. And once I'm finished with a story I can't recall much more than the characters' names."

He closed the booklet and leaned back in his chair before he spoke. "You do know that you are famous, don't you? I looked you up once. Not you, but Miss Blackwell. She...you are world known not only for the series that your family is reading, but also for the donations you've made to schools and libraries. And the fact that no one knows anything about you."

She flushed. "I don't even know how they found out I did that. I swear no one wants to keep secrets anymore." She looked up at him as he continued to stare at her. "You're about to tell me that I have to tell them, aren't you?"

"I think it'll come out, yes. I'm sure that your other lawyer is right now making plans to let someone in his office know and they'll tell someone else until the right someone gets the story. How do you want me to handle it?"

"You'll be my lawyer then?" She didn't realize how much she'd needed to hear him say that.

"Of course I will. It will be a pleasure." He sat up again. "We'll have to tell Janice. She'll need to know, then you'd better make the rest of the family aware. Things are about to get a whole lot more public for you."

She nodded. "I know. But I don't...I'm terrified."

Janice came in and he told her to have a seat and nodded at Jazzie.

So she told the first person she knew that wasn't on a need-to-know basis. Well, she thought with a smile, other than Nathan. And telling him hadn't been her idea either, but now that he knew she was glad for it. So far he'd not told anyone and she knew that he was close to Drew.

Janice took it well. Jazzie wasn't sure if it had to do with her professionalism or that she didn't believe her, but she got right to work on setting up a press conference and a meeting with the head of HBO. Things were moving at an alarming rate and, before long, Drew was setting up a luncheon with her family for today. Jazzie was suddenly very terrified.

"Take deep breaths. If it helps, I didn't invite your mother." She looked up at him grinning. "Yeah, I figured that'd help. It's going to be fine, love. You can't believe that any of them will be nothing but happy for you."

She hoped he was right. A few minutes after nine, and two hours after she'd walked into her new lawyer's office, she was walking toward Nathan's to see him. His note had told her to come there after her meeting and he'd make it worth her while. His secretary told her to go in after she'd buzzed him. Jazzie pressed her hand to her belly and went in.

~~~

Nathan had never done what he was about to do with a woman before. He'd worked all morning in setting this up and hoped it wouldn't backfire. When she walked in he could tell she was surprised. He had to smile at the slight flare of disappointment when she'd seen what he'd done.

The blanket on the floor was covered with small containers. He'd wanted to have a picnic with her and knew that it was too chilly, especially in early April, for them to have one. The rain had also stopped it, but only in the setting. He'd set up the food to be delivered today by calling in a favor on his way into work. His friend had been more than happy to send him a basket of goodies.

"I thought you'd skip breakfast and wanted you to have something to power you through the day." He kissed her lightly and led her to the repast. "I didn't know what you'd like so I had him send over a little bit of everything. Also, I got some of that tea you like to drink."

She looked at him from across the blanket and he noticed the tears. Before he could say anything, she told him she was fine. "No one had ever done anything like this for me before. I don't know what to say. It's lovely."

He sat her on the edge of the blanket and began opening some of the food. Tony, his friend, had gone to the extreme, but he was happy. There were small bowls of fruit; cantaloupe, grapes, and honeydew. There was a container of strawberries and another of soft chocolate. When he opened one of the larger containers, it was to find meats and cheeses and a long sleeve of delicate crackers. There were other items as well; mustard that Nathan knew the restaurant that Tony owned was famous for, silver knives, and china plates. Long stem glasses and a bottle of very nice champagne. The last large container he opened held an assortment of small thin slices of cheesecake and chocolate truffles.

"This is so lovely," she told him as he fed her a grape. "I feel like one of those beautiful women in those romance movies that meets her lover for an afternoon of decadent pleasure."

"If your smile is any indication I would say that you may have your own romance movie soon." He fed her a piece of cheese on a cracker. "So did he make fun of you and tell you you were a hack?"

She flushed slightly. When he'd told her to go to Drew last night she'd told him that she was worried that he'd throw her out of his office. She said that she didn't believe that she was all that good and believed completely that he would see her for the fraud she was.

"No. He didn't even blink an eye. He did say that Quinn said the sex scenes were the best she'd ever read. I got the feeling that he benefited from those scenes just a little." He

76

could tell she had more to say. "Drew is setting up a press conference for day after tomorrow. And I have a meeting with my family today at two. He said that it'll be out soon who I am and that I should tell them before it comes out in the paper."

Nathan nodded. He figured that Drew would do that. The other lawyer that she'd had told her that she was stupid for dropping him, that he'd been the best thing that had ever happened to her. She'd been so upset after talking to the man that Nathan wanted to hunt the guy down and beat the shit out of him.

"I want you there," she said quietly. "I want to tell them that we are seeing each other…unless you'd rather we kept this, whatever we're having, quiet?"

He wanted to shout it to the world that Nathan Allen Howard the Forth had his sub, but he was reasonably sure that's not what she meant. He picked up another cracker before he answered her. "What it is you want?" He held up his hand before she answered. "You know what I am. What I'll always be. And I'm sure that now that you'll be public people are going to be doing some major back stories on you. You don't need to see *'Famous Author Sleeps With Drug Addict'* spread across the headlines."

She smiled at him. "No, I don't. But I wouldn't mind seeing, *'Famous Author has Gorgeous Man Tie Her Up and Make Her Scream Her Release Every Night,'* though."

"You do scream very loudly when you come. Do you know how hard it makes me when you do that? My cock aches to be inside of you right now." He watched her eyes darken. "The way that you tighten around me, my tongue or my cock, makes me want to feel you come again and again."

She moaned his name as she moved closer to him. He wanted her now, wanted her to lie down, and he wanted to fuck her hard. She opened her blouse and he felt his cock jerk in his pants. He stopped her with his hand on hers.

"I can't. Not right now at any rate." Her moan made him want to tell her he'd changed his mind. "I have a meeting in twenty minutes. Not near enough time to do all the things I'm thinking about right now."

She moved his hand away and reached for his belt. "Like what? Like me sucking on your cock again? I need to do that right now. I want to feel you coming down the back of my throat again."

He leaned back and let her open his fly. He wanted her in the worst way and couldn't seem to stop her from taking him. When she freed his cock and wrapped her lips around him he moaned. Christ, this woman was going to kill him.

"Wait. I want you to lay over me." He pulled her dress up and over her hips as she settled over his head when he was flat on his back. "We're going to do this so we both get something out of it. But you can't scream." When he was on his back he turned her so that her pussy was over his mouth. He licked his way up her thigh.

"I wanted this since I put this on this morning. I thought about you, thought about you taking me across your desk and fucking me until I couldn't walk. But I like this better." She reached for his cock. "Let me suck you dry."

He buried his face in her thighs and felt her mouth wrap around him. He rocked into her mouth as he sucked her clit. She was hot, soaking wet, and he knew that he wasn't going to last. Even as he fucked her luscious mouth, he knew that he was going to have to bring some toys to the office so that the next time she came in, he'd have her on his desk. He couldn't wait to lean her over it and pound her tight ass while he tugged at her pussy.

It only took a few strokes and lesser suckles at her clit. Her climax had her tightening her thighs around his ears as he came hard into her mouth. Her moan rippled along his cock, making his eyes cross. Christ, he thought as he rolled over and then pulled her lax body over his, she was going to kill   him.

Chapter 9

The meeting was held in her favorite local restaurant. She figured Drew had set it up this way so that she'd be less nervous. She wasn't. Jazzie was pretty sure that at any moment she was going to throw up. She smoothed her hands down over her dress again and took a deep breath. This was going to be fine.

The dress had arrived today while she was in the Howard building. The UPS man knew to put things in the garage; he'd done it for her often enough. But this package couldn't have come at a better time. Her sister could make killer clothes and Jazzie so needed a boost right now.

It was a shade of blue so intense, so brilliant, that it probably didn't have a name. And instead of taking away from the wearer, it suited her perfectly. The top was a tight bodice that had no sleeves of any sort. The short jacket in the same bright hue concealed the fact that her boobs were barely covered and drew the eye, instead, to the long line of her body while toning down the ample size of her breasts. She loved the short skirt of the dress, the silky material gathered at her hips in a fanlike pattern. The length of the dress was almost illegal, but she loved it. It made her feel sexy and alive, made her wish that she'd not needed its boost and could have shown it off for Nathan tonight.

"Do you know what this is about?" her brother asked her. "I don't mind us all getting together, but I'm curious. Drew only said there was a big announcement to make."

"Yes. But I'm not going to tell you until everyone else comes in. Go away, Cain." She pushed him a little and all she managed to do was make him grin at her. "You're not going to be able to get this out of me, so just give it up."

"Ah come on, Jazzie. You know you want to tell me. Just like when we were kids. You never could keep things from your big brother. Tell me now and I'll be all surprised when the announcement is made."

She walked away. She had kept her secret for this long, a few more minutes wasn't going to kill her. She didn't think so anyway. She looked at her watch again. Nathan had told her he was in a meeting until late, but he'd be there for her. She hoped so; she could use a friendly face.

"Okay, everyone is here. I think we should order first and then make the announcement." Drew handed her a sheet of paper. "I hope you don't mind, but I made up something for you to say. This way, if you get too nervous, you can just read from this." She glanced down at it, but didn't really read it. "Nathan just called. He said to turn on your phone and that he was on his way. Are you and him…"

"Yes. I thought I'd open with that." Jazzie grinned at his surprised expression. "Not very long and it's nothing serious. We just…well, he's my… Yes. We're seeing each other." She so didn't want to get into him being her Master and her his sub right now. Nor did she think Drew would appreciate her telling him that they'd had the most incredible sex not three hours ago. She glanced up at the door when Nathan appeared. She didn't think Drew would be happy to learn that her thighs were soaked because she was in love with her sister-in-law's step brother. Nathan kissed her on the mouth and closed any and all conversation on how she wanted to tell her family. They pretty much got it.

The wait staff came in and took their order. Jazzie's belly was so upset she didn't want to order, but Nathan had taken her menu from her and ordered for her. She only hoped that whatever it was, she'd be able to hold it down until she got home. Drew stood up and picked up his water glass and knife.

After gently hitting the knife to the crystal, he cleared his throat. "I'm so glad you all could make it today on such short notice. I think that you'll all be happy with the announcements that I have to share with you. First and foremost, I took on a client today. I think that I'll have more fun with this one than I've had in a while. But first, Jazzie has something to say."

He sat as she stood up. She was shaking all over. This was her family; they loved her, she kept telling herself. She looked over at Alyssa when she burst out laughing.

"If this is you and Nathan you want to tell us about, I want to be the first to say congratulations. I've never seen either of you happier. Is this about a wedding?"

"No," Jazzie said quickly. "I mean, no. We've only just…that is, we're just…" She looked at Nathan. "We are taking things at our own pace. But that's not why I had Drew ask you to come here. I'm…that is to say, I have a…I didn't think it would…oh shit. I'm Jasmine Blackwell and HBO has approached me about a series deal on my series. And because I fired my lawyer this morning Nathan suggested that I ask Drew to help me."

She sat down. There wasn't a sound around the table. Even the children seemed to know something monumental had just happened. Nathan held her hand under the table and gave her a tight squeeze when the silence seemed to stretch on.

"*The* Jasmine Blackwell? The books that…you're Jasmine Blackwell?" Alyssa leaned over and put her tattered copy of her book, *Willow,* on the table. "This is yours?"

"Yes. I wrote that one about a year ago. There are five more books in the series. The next one, *Midnight,* comes out in about six weeks."

"But you never said anything. You've been writing my favorite books for..." Quinn flushed as she continued. "Christ, how long have you been doing this anyway?"

"Since ninth grade, but only on the market since you graduated from high school. I've been really lucky." Her family looked angry. "I never meant to become this great writer. Hell, I'm not so sure why you guys even like my stories. They were..."

"They were what?" Nathan asked her softly. "Tell them what you told me. They were what?"

She looked him in the eye as she spoke. "They were the only way I could escape at times. The only way I could...cope. There were times I could escape for hours, sometimes days creating love and romance for the people in my head. I made things for them that I wanted, what I needed to make the stuff going on around me so much...less."

She heard the applause. It startled her at first when she looked at Payton. He stood up and continued what he was doing. Soon Sin got up, came around the table, and hugged her tightly before she too started to clap. She started to ask them what the hell was wrong with them when Shamus spoke.

"Honey, I'm really proud of you. It couldn't have been easy trying to deal. With the things that Lilliane has told me it's small wonder you had to do something to survive. But Jasmine Blackwell?" He looked over at Nathan with a huge grin. "Way to go, man. You must love helping her work out all those love scenes."

"Hey," Cain shouted. "If you don't mind, she *is* my sister. I *so* don't want to think about her having...she is not having sex. None of you are. Do you understand me? Not one of you."

Sin kissed him on the head as she walked by him. "Of course we aren't. And I'm sure you aren't either. I almost feel sorry for poor Alyssa, but her not having to endure sex with you could be a blessing. Connor was born how now?"

The table became much like their dinners of late. Loud with laughter and conversation, the sounds of children and adults alike having fun. She looked back over at Nathan as he squeezed her hand.

"They didn't make fun of me," she told him, awestruck with the realization. "They seemed very happy about it."

"Of course they are. They love you very much." He leaned in to her neck and bit her. "I know you more than likely don't want to hear this now, but I'm in love with you too. I think I have been for some time, but was afraid."

She pulled back from his words whispered at her ear. She was so shocked she could barely speak. Before she could wrap her mouth around a single syllable the food arrived. Too overwhelmed to do much more than play with her salad she kept thinking about what he'd said. She didn't realize her sister Quinn was seated next to her until she handed her Alba. She looked to her other side and saw that Nathan had moved to where Payton and Shamus sat with Cain.

"Feels pretty good, huh?" Before she could ask Quinn what she meant she went on. "I know that when I figured out I was in love with Drew all I wanted to do was hide it from him and the rest of you guys. But it doesn't work."

"He loves me. How is that even…why?" She flushed when her sister laughed. "I don't think this is funny. He just told me that he loves me and now what am I supposed to do?"

"Love him back," Alyssa said as she sat down across from her. "I know that I'm a poor one to give advice, but you've no idea how relentless they can be when they get it in their head they love you. I tried to shake Cain for weeks before he wore me down. Just give in and figure out that you can love him too."

Jazzie looked down at Nathan who looked at her at the same time. He winked at her and she felt her body respond as though he'd touched her. She looked back at her sisters as Sin sat down with them.

"I do. Love him, I mean. I've been in love with him since he started working for you. But I never...I was trying to tell myself that I'd be happy with him just from afar. But...I guess I was fooling myself."

Alyssa nodded. "Really? I never...he must have had feelings for you too if the way he looks at you now is any indication. He looks at you like you're Thanksgiving dinner and Christmas morning all rolled into one."

They laughed as the restaurant staff began to clear away the plates and extra glasses. Quinn cleared her throat as the last fork was cleared away. "I was wondering...what kind of family discount do we get now that we know? And don't forget that my husband is now your lawyer."

~~~

Ginny put all the money back under her mattress and frowned. Something wasn't right. She couldn't quite put her finger on it, but she just knew it. She walked around her room again and looked at the small traps she'd put out. None of them were sprung.

The small piece of tape she'd put over her drawers wasn't moved on any of them. She looked over the closet and saw that, other than dust, the string she'd put there to show that someone had opened her door was still on the outside of it rather on the inside. She'd seen that trick on some show a few weeks ago.

The guy had thought his kids were stealing his drugs and had hung a small thread over the closet frame. When the person opened the door the thread would drape inside where his stash was instead of the outside.

The money was there as well. The bags were a little moved around, but nothing she could prove that wasn't because she'd been sleeping like crap for the past two weeks. Ginny picked up the brown paper bag of the money she'd just pulled out from under the mattress.

Ten grand was what this one was going to cost her. Well, that and the money she'd promised him at the end. He'd wanted sex, but she told him that was out of the question. She was saving herself for someone else. She had no idea why he thought that was funny, but she ignored him as best she could. She was to meet him in one hour.

The guy, Tank something, had told her that he would have it done by end of next week. She had told him the girls' habits and had given him all the information she had on Jazzie. The girl was as habitual as anyone she knew. Tank told her that those type of people, he called her lazy, were best to get rid of. They "mucked it up" for the rest of the human race. Ginny wasn't sure she'd call this guy human, more sub human than anything.

He was huge for one thing. Not like a fat-man-gone-crane-needed-to-move huge, but bigger. She wondered if, when this sucker died, and she couldn't help but think it would be real soon, would they have a casket on hand or would they need to hope someone would buy a piano and use the box it came in.

But he came with a lot of references and, of all things, a portfolio. She'd been both aghast and excited at what he'd done to some of his victims. And the pictures were put into a photo album like some of Guinevere's friends did with their grandkiddies. Ginny had been particularly impressed with the way he'd made each of them look like they'd offed themselves rather than someone had paid him to take them out.

"This one is my favorite," he'd told her of one really gory shot. "The wife had needed some quick cash to leave the country and… well, let's just say I provided her with the funds to do so. The poor bastard didn't know what hit him. That bad case of the flu had been a stroke of good luck and the guy that I acquired it from didn't fare any better."

She didn't really care how he took her out. She just wanted her gone. Ginny was also thinking that they were going about this all wrong. She thought once she got rid of Jasmine Zinnia, as her mother called her, then she'd just start taking them out two or three at a time. They were multiplying faster than she could take care of them.

Money. It was all she could think about now. All that lovely money. The first thing she was going to do was to move into that big house. She wanted that house and all those maids and shit. Ginny wanted to wake up every morning and have breakfast in bed then go to bed every night with satin and silk sheets to sleep on. She'd been putting in a lot of time on this and felt as if she deserved it.

She took a cab over to the building she was to meet Tank at. The stupid car hadn't started again. She wasn't sure how to get it replaced; she wasn't spending her money on it. If Guinevere wanted something to get around in then she could fucking ask Cain. Or, she thought with a sly smile, let her fuck Cain and he'd buy her one. Oh, she wanted that man.

Ginny had first seen Cain when he'd been a teenager. He'd been helping one of his fucked up sisters with a battered face. She'd found out later that Roscoe had beaten his kids all the time and she hooked up with him to get close to the boy. But Cain had moved out not long after. He'd gotten some sort of educational loan or some shit and she'd only get to see him if Guinevere let her. That was another thing she planned to take care of—Guinevere.

The woman had to go. She was nothing but a stick in the mud and Ginny felt she was holding her back from doing what really needed to be done. Ginny had never met a more whiny person in all her life. And the fact that she'd left all the issues concerning the money and the money-grubbing whore for her to take care of didn't set well with Ginny. Yes, as soon as possible Guinevere had to go away.

Tank was leaning against the wall when she stepped inside the building. Ginny had the horrible urge to giggle, wondering if the building was going to withstand his weight or would it come tumbling down on them both as they talked?

"Been watching that girl. You know she's got some man living with her most nights? Gonna make it a bit harder to get to her with him hanging around, you know," he said as she handed him the money. "Might have to give you a two-fer."

"Give me or charge me for the two of them? I don't give two shits about his ass. If you take him out, then it's going to be on your own dime, not mine. The girl needs to be dead. How you do it or who you take out with her is none of my concern." She watched as he thumbed through the money with his fat fingers. "I'll give you the rest when you finish the job and no one points their fingers at me."

"I'm a pro-fess-i-nell." She hated the way he stretched out that one word like it was supposed to be funny. Professional what, is what she wanted to ask him. Eater?

"See that you are. Do you have any idea when you might make the hit?" She loved that term, it sounded so evil. "I want her gone and if you do a good job with this one, I'll use you in the other hits I have planned. I want them all gone."

He looked at her sharply and she was suddenly unsure of him. Was he a hit man or an undercover cop? She didn't break eye contact with him, but waited for him to look away first. She wasn't sure why, but felt that if she had done so he would have lost respect for her as a killer. That made her feel so much better that she simply forgot about him possibly being undercover. Besides, who the fuck would hire someone as big as he was anyway?

They talked for an hour more. He tried to convince her that she could get a good discount if she sucked him off and she assured him there wasn't enough of a discount for her to do that even if he were to give her the money back. She wanted to ask him if he'd even seen his dick in a while, but didn't. She was afraid he'd try to whip it out and she was worried about his health. She wanted him to work this through first then he could die any fucking time he wanted.

Ginny waited for the cab to pick her up again and walked to the little cafe she'd seen there several weeks ago. It was a nice place that served hot coffee in real cups and donuts that gave you a sugar rush that lasted most of the day. She was sitting at a small table by the window when she saw a paper lying open on the table across from her.

The money-grubbing whore was on the front page. There was this long article about how she and Ginny's Cain had donated some god-awful amount of money to some stupid halfway house for ex-cons. Ginny snorted. The only thing that ex-cons needed was a chance to get at the bitch's money, not some house where they were being taught the way things were going to be from now on and to be told that they needed to stay out of prison. Really? No shit, dumb ass. She knew that Roscoe hadn't been in one of those houses and he'd turned out all right. If the whore had given him the money he'd still be alive right now.

By the time her cab came to get her she was pissed again. She needed to get these people gone so that she could show these cock-suckers what to do with all that cash. She wouldn't be donating any of it to anyone unless it was to a charity of her own. She was getting into the cab when she thought of a perfect name. *"I Fucking Did it My Way and Still Came Out Smelling Like a Rose Charity."*

Chapter 10

Jasmine Blackwell was outted the next morning.

Jazzie was glad that Nathan had spent the night when she opened the paper the next morning and read the headline. Didn't these people have anything better to report as the top news story, she wondered? The length of the article made her cringe and Nathan turned from cooking their breakfast when she moaned.

"At least they spelled your name right." She glared at him and he laughed. "Look, you knew this was going to happen. At least now your family will be there for you."

She looked back at the bold headline. HBO WANTS OUR JASMINE BLACKWELL'S BOOKS. She wondered when she'd become their *Jasmine,* but simply read the story out loud to Nathan.

"'Jasmine Waite, our own little shy girl, has just announced that she is *the* Jasmine Blackwell, author of the naughty books *The Main Characters*. Miss Waite could not be reached for comment.'" She looked up from the first paragraph. "That's because Miss Waite wasn't privy to this thing." She continued reading when Nathan kissed her nose. "'Couldn't be reached for comment to talk about the HBO series that they want to run on her books this fall.' I wasn't aware they'd set a date yet," she told Nathan as he set a plate of waffles in front of her.

"Could be they're making that up. I'd call Drew when you're done and see what he has to say. HBO may have contacted the other lawyer with a date and he didn't tell them you had fired him."

She wrote it on the pad of paper she always had on her. She tossed the paper on the counter as she dug into her food. She was just eating the last sliced ham he'd fried for her when her phone rang. Nathan answered it as he walked by it from the refrigerator.

"Yes, she's here. I'm not sure, but I can ask... No, that won't be... Yes, I'm sure you are, but that doesn't... Yes. Hang on, let me find out." He winked at her before he put the phone on mute. "You're going to be very popular, it seems. The ladies club at the library wants to know if you'll do them the honor of coming to their luncheon tomorrow. They want to talk to you about your writing career."

She groaned. "This is why I never wanted anyone to find out. No, I don't want to do lunch with those old biddies. They wouldn't even let me have a library card when I was a kid because my father, and I quote, 'wouldn't have the money to pay for the books I wouldn't return.' Like I was going to steal the books from them or something." She glared at him again when he laughed.

"Look, you knew this was going to happen. You had to know that people were going to change their minds about how they treated you. I have the same thing. Now that Alyssa and I are close, it seems that everyone I partied with before now thinks I'm as rich as her. I'm not." He handed her the phone. "You can be famous and gracious or you can be famous and a bitch. Up to you. I'll love you either way."

She felt her heart rate leap. They'd sort of not talked about what he'd said to her in the restaurant yesterday. She took the phone and stuck her tongue out at him.

She ended up agreeing to go. She also agreed that she'd sign books that any of them wanted to bring in as well. The phone rang as soon as she hung up. It was the bookstore in town. Could she see her way to come in and do a book signing soon? They would have all her books on display by the following Monday. Could she see her way to come in on Friday? She had to go to her office and pull up her calendar to see. By the time she'd made arrangements for that gig, her phone rang twice more while she was marking the date. She let the first one go to voicemail and the second she answered.

"So you were going to call me today and tell me, right?" Gracie said in way of greeting. "My own sister is some famous smut writer and I have to read about it online. Shame on you for not sharing."

"Oh like you aren't famous. And I write. I don't design these incredible clothes that actresses and queens beg you for. Didn't I see one of your creations on a Golden Globe winner a few weeks back?' Jazzie smiled when her sister snorted.

"So? You know I do that. I, however, did not know about you. Why is that, I wonder? And it says in this article that you and a certain man are fucking like bunnies." Jazzie sat up quickly in her chair and didn't realize her sister was joking until she nearly killed herself trying to find the paper. "So, you going to tell me about him or do I have to read between the lines?"

She sighed. She and Gracie were close. They being the only singles in their family, they'd bonded like none of the others needed them to. Quinn and Cain had that special twin bond that was freaky and Sin and Lilliane were identical twins that seemed to be able to read each other without speaking. Gracie and she had had to rely on spoken words and each other. They had protected each other as kids.

"It's Nathan Howard, Alyssa's brother. And before you ask, I'm not giving you details about our sex life." Jazzie laughed at her sister's cussing. "You'll have to read about them in the next books. He's very good at sex."

They talked for another ten minutes before Jazzie had to go and see Nathan off. He'd cleaned up the kitchen while she'd been busy on the phone. She enjoyed him holding her, enjoyed him just being there.

"I was wondering if you'd like to have dinner with me tonight?" he asked. "I want us to have more than just sex. Not that I won't molest you under the table, but we could also have something to eat while we do it. Besides, it's been a dream of mine to make you come in a room full of people."

She felt her pussy drench. When he leaned in and took her mouth she moaned at his touch. This man could make her go from zero to ninety in less than a heartbeat. He turned them around and pressed her against the counter. He rocked into her and she moaned again. When he pulled away she whimpered.

"You are making me hard, woman. What the hell am I going to do to you to make you behave?"

"Fuck me?" she asked hopefully. "I know you have to go to work, but know that I'm writing two scenes in two different books today and I'm going to think of you when I do them. I love the way your cock moves inside of me, Nathan."

He growled at her and swatted her ass. Who would have ever thought that something so painful could feel so delicious? She walked him to the door and kissed him again before he went to his car. She nearly had the door closed when he came back. She was pulled to him so quickly that she nearly fell. His kiss was hungry and demanding and she gave as much as he took.

"Come by the office. I want to lay you over my desk and taste you. Then I want to take you hard and fast with the door unlocked." He kissed her again and, before she could speak, he was gone.

Her phone rang all day. She finally had to turn the ringer off and send a text message to her family. She told them if they needed her to call her cell phone, that she wasn't taking anymore calls. Drew texted her ten minutes later. And she called him right back.

"HBO did contact the other lawyer," he informed her after he asked if she had time to talk for a bit. "I have it cleared up now. And you will be meeting with them sometime tomorrow. By the way, can you hook me up to your personal calendar so that we don't overlap each other in schedules? Nathan was in my office and told me about the library thing. Also, you'll need to hire someone to answer phones for you. Got anyone in mind?"

It was moving too fast. She'd gone from weird sister to famous author in less than two days and her head was spinning. She laid her head on her desk and took several deep breaths before she answered, Drew's concerned calling of her name. "I'm here. I'm not sure… What would I ask of someone? And I don't even have an office. I don't even… Drew, I'm freaking out here." His laughter made her smile. "I'm a little overwhelmed here."

"I can hear that. How about I look into an office for you? Alyssa has three buildings downtown and I could maybe get one of the simple offices for you. You could go there once a week or have whoever answers the phones to courier them to you. It would also be a great place to have meetings like the one I'm setting up for HBO to come to."

She marked her list of things to do and wondered how the hell she was supposed to do all this and write. She said as much to him.

"That's why you need help. I'll get someone from our staff to fill in until you find someone. There are a few contract things I'd like to ask you about before we go into this other deal."

"I want you to meet my publisher. I called her this morning and she is willing to meet you anytime." She hit send on her calendar that she'd made him administrator on. "You should have full access to my events thing. Also, just set things up whenever you think, but not on the dates that are in pink. Those are the days that I go to the shelter for Alyssa."

"Got it. Not very full, but I expect that to change before long." She groaned. He laughed. "I promise this will get better."

"I hope so because not having time to write could make me very crazy. Just make sure that you don't book me anything too much. I'm not...I'm not a very good people person."

He told her he'd take care of her. Then he brought up her contacts with Chastity Midland of Midland World Publishing. He asked her to send them to him so he could go over them. She told him she was happy with Chastity, but he assured her that he only wanted to see what they said. She sent them to him as well.

"Okay, darling. If you're out and about today, come by my office. I want you to see what the offices I have in mind for you look like and then we'll set you up with a couple of people working here. You should be able to find someone, even if it's only for the short term."

Chapter 11

Guinevere waited for Ginny to show up the next morning. She'd had enough and wanted to know where the money had come from and what she was planning to do with it. She had an idea that it was for making her family pay, but there were things they could be doing with that much money and it was just sitting under the mattress. Then she picked up the paper again.

There was no way that her stupid daughter could be the person they were making her out to be. The girl could barely pay attention. How on earth did they think that she could string a bunch of words together enough to make a story? And especially not the kind of story that these people at the paper were saying that she wrote, whatever the hell *contemporary romance* was.

It also said she had an office to be opened soon in one of the Howard buildings. That money-grubbing whore was supplying stupid Jasmine Zinnia with an office in one of her precious buildings, but she couldn't spare a bigger place for her mother-in-law? She needed to talk with Cain. This had been going on long enough.

"I agree. What do you think we've been working on now for the past three years? Do you think this has been a blast for me to plan, all this while you sit back and be the good girl?" Guinevere looked up in the reflection to see

Ginny. "And going to talk to Cain will be a total waste of your time. Let me go."

"You'd only get him pissed again. It was hard enough getting him to calm down after you went in to see about your foot. He said you made a pass at him." Guinevere had been mortified when Cain had told her that he didn't appreciate her acting like that and that if she did anything like it again, he'd refuse to see her. "He was mad enough that he said he'd cut us off. He told her that mothers did not act like that to their sons. He was really pissed off. You have to leave him alone." Ginny only snorted. Guinevere held up the paper so she could see it. "Do you believe that this is Jasmine Zinnia? I certainly don't. The girl just managed to graduate high school for all her daydreaming. And now they expect us to believe she's this famous author. Not fucking likely."

"Maybe she has one of those ghost writers. You know, this other person writes the stories and Jazzie takes all the credit. I read about it in one of the magazines at the end of the rack. The real writer sued the bitch for all her money and won. I think we should look into that for the future. Could be you could claim to be the real author and we could take more of her estate when she's dead."

Guinevere doubted that she'd be able to pull it off, but didn't say anything. She tossed one of the bags of money on the floor and glared at Ginny. She was determined not to be the one who asked questions, but have Ginny explain herself. The other woman simply glared back.

"You should know that I found it a few days ago and hoped you'd explain it to me without me having to ask." Ginny still didn't speak. "I don't like that you're withholding things from me. And I want to know where you got all this money."

The smile was scary. "From the whore, of course. I found someone to help me at her office who is skimming big bucks off her. The bitch doesn't even have a clue that it's happening. And when she figures it out, she'll think it's that fucking drunk brother of hers. Never saw a more useless person than him." Ginny smiled again. "Of course it helps that the person in Atlanta has more of a drug and drink problem than her fucktard brother."

Guinevere nodded, still not understanding, but she didn't want to appear stupid again. But she did wonder how they were ending up with the money if the person at the other end of the United States was stealing it. She was ready to ask when Ginny spoke again.

"The guy owes me a favor. And with my connections I've been able to set him up with a higher grade coke than what he can get on his own. Kinda like he scratches my back and I feed his habit." Ginny laughed again. "The brother, the druggy, lets the accounting department know what he spends on that project that Whore gave him to play with and he keeps all the receipts. Once he sends them to the Atlanta firm for processing, my boy down there makes some…let's call them creative, adjustments on them. Then he sends me the difference."

Guinevere was impressed. She told Ginny so. She wished at times she could think things through like that, something clever, but all she'd be able to do would be to get caught. But she did have a question. "How are you cashing the checks? There has to be some way for them to trace them back to you, right?" Ginny was shaking her head. "He surely doesn't send you cash, does he?"

"Yeah. He thinks if he sends me a check I'd only have to save a copy to get his ass in trouble if something happens. Thing is, he thinks he's got me 'cause of the post office box I use. They aren't going to find anything there because I have several of them. And each one of them has someone who collects it and mails it to the next and then the next until it's been all over the place before it gets to me. He's got no clue."

101

"So you have a post office box in other places and they simply forward it on to you from there?" Ginny nodded. Guinevere was impressed again, but didn't say so. Giving Ginny a big head would be a mistake. She'd only lord it over Guinevere for months how much smarter she was than Guinevere and that just wouldn't do.

When Ginny finally went away Guinevere sat staring at the paper again. She knew that Ginny was smarter, but she didn't think she was right on this account. Jasmine Zinnia wasn't smart enough to pull this off without some help. Guinevere wondered if maybe Ginny was in on it with her trying to make her mother look bad, but doubted that almost as soon as she thought it. Guinevere decided to take a trip to her office and see for herself. She called her phone to get the address and see if she'd buy her lunch when the call went directly to voicemail. Well, she'd simply go over there.

Gathering up her jacket and purse, Guinevere picked up the hefty bag of cash that was still on the floor. She'd counted it and found just over twenty grand in the bags and all in small to larger bills. She opened the bag and took out three fifties and five twenties. Maybe she'd buy her daughter lunch. It would be a good way to make nice with her to get her to follow her wherever Ginny needed her to. Smiling for the first time in days Guinevere hobbled out of the house and to the car and took it as a good sign that it started on the first try.

~~~

Jazzie looked around the "simple" office, as Drew had called it. It was huge. Not only that, but it was frigging huge. She laughed at herself at that. She looked over at the woman who'd been showing her around.

"There is a conference room just off your own office and there is a large in-suite bath, as well as two regular baths for guests. The kitchen has access to the room and can provide luncheon for up to twenty-five people." Jazzy looked over at Nathan who had agreed to come with her as the woman pointed out the other rooms. "This room is for private conferences, up to five or so people. There are projectors in each room, by the way, and a state of the art sound system."

"I have that in my office as well," Drew told her. "I didn't think it would be anything I'd use, but it has come in handy when trying to show a group of people what you're talking about."

Jazzie looked over the round table with the six chairs around it. The furniture was beautiful and the chairs looked like she could take a nap in them and not wake up sore. She grinned at the thought. She'd not been getting a great deal of sleep lately, not that she was complaining, but she was staring to lag a bit. She looked over at Nathan, the reason for her lack of sleep, and listened to him ask about the secretary that Drew said was coming today.

"She should be here within the hour. I was under the impression that she will only be temporary until you have a chance to interview someone else," Mrs. Dunlap said as she waved her hand toward another door. "I know Lucy Rosedale and I think she is a very reliable and very competent woman. She also, if you don't mind me saying, should be able to keep all the...undesirables out of your office."

"Undesirables? I'm not sure I know what—"

"Oh, Miss, I only meant people who would be wanting more than your autograph. You know the type? People who would come in and try and get to your lovely self and all your money. Not to mention...well, I've read your books and I must say...well, men, miss. Men will do most anything if they think a pretty girl might want to act out what they read in your books."

Jazzie flushed and refused to look at Nathan. They'd been playing last night with a particular scene that had been giving her fits. She felt her skin heat when she remembered her own suggestions on what she might do to improve what they'd been doing. She knew the moment he noticed her discomfort. His soft, sexy laugh shimmered along her skin as his fingers did when he touched her, leaving her breathless and heated.

"Here is your office, miss. There is someone at the door out front. The security guard said he'd let me know when someone arrived. If you'll be alright for a few minutes, I'll go and see to it." Jazzie nodded as Mrs. Dunlap walked away.

She opened the door to her office and stopped. "Christ," she murmured under her breath and heard Nathan chuckle. She moved forward slowly and walked to the desk.

The building had been decorated, she'd been told. Alyssa had told her that she'd only just had the basics done in the other offices, but with one she'd finished. She said she wanted a room that others, would-be renters, would be able to see potential in. This room screamed potential, Jazzie thought with a laugh, and money.

The walls were done in creamy white paper that had pinstripes of silver shot through it. The chair board and the light oak paneling at the bottom half gleamed in richness. The oak wood design was throughout the room, but more so in the shelves on two of the four walls.

They were filled with small mementos one would probably collect on a vacation as well as a plethora of framed pictures. The small touches gave the room appeal and warmth. The other two walls, one of which was floor to ceiling windows, gave the whole room a brightness and warmth that the fireplace against the wall would never be able to match. Jazzie picked up one of the framed pictures on the large desk and laughed. She handed it to Nathan when he came up behind her.

"Someone wants you to have this office as your own, I think," he told her as he set the picture back on the desk. "I think I saw her take that when we had your luncheon the other day."

It was a picture of the two of them together, her and Nathan. Alyssa had taken it with her phone. And if memory served, then the next three pictures were of Jazzie holding the triples, then Connor and Tonya.

"I think so." She wandered around the room more, touching things and picking up frames to see if she knew any of the people. Some she did; others she didn't. She sat on Nathan's lap when he sat in the office chair.

"It's a big office, isn't it?" He nodded and slid his hand up under her skirt. "Nathan, there are people just down the—" His fingers dug deep into her. "Yes, Master," was all she could manage.

"I wanted to see if you were wet. And now that I know, all I can think about is taking you right here to see if you can be quiet." He bit her shoulder and she shivered. "You didn't do so well the other night and now we can't go back there."

He'd taken her to dinner and he'd molested her under the table like he said he was going to do. What she didn't expect him to do was touch her with a small vibrator. The little rabbit, as it was called, had zeroed in on her clit and caught her off guard. She came with a loud shout. Nathan had explained to everyone that she'd had a fright, but they didn't hang around to explain. She was certain that every person in that room knew just what she'd been doing.

"Lean over and let me taste you. Don't come. I want you to keep quiet and let me have my fill of your sweet pussy." She didn't even hesitate, but stood and leaned over, bracing her hands on the desk. Her skirt lifted over her hips. His growl made her moan.

He separated her ass cheeks and nipped at her. She wanted to feel his mouth there, but didn't speak. He hadn't

105

told her that she couldn't, but she was almost afraid to. She wasn't sure that she could speak and try not to come at the same time. His terse "turn around" made her pussy gush more and she sat on the desk when he told her to.

He positioned her feet up on the arms of the chair. She was wide open for him now and could see that he was pleased with what he saw. She leaned back and waited for him to take her. She knew that Mrs. Dunlap could be back at any second and knew that this was part of the thrill they both enjoyed.

He stood up and she was sure that he was going to either lock the door or fuck her. She waited for either, wanted either. He pulled her hips to the edge and reached for his zipper. She knew that he was commando under the trousers he had on and couldn't wait to see his thick cock. She licked her lips in anticipation. He reached into the opening and watched as he stroked his cock. Her pussy was so wet, so ready for him, she was sure that she was going to ruin the beautiful wood. But he stepped back a step. Then another until he was too far away to touch her.

Her heart pounded as he removed his hand and then zipped up. She looked up at him when he helped her stand and smoothed her skirt back down. She was trembling with need and she couldn't move. He leaned in and whispered in her ear just as she heard voices down the hall.

"When I tell you to lean back you will and not before." The smart smack to her ass nearly made her cry out, but a look from him silenced her. "You will obey or be punished. I'm going to go back to my office and slick up my cock with lotion and come all over myself thinking about how hot you looked laying before me. Next time." He kissed her. "Next time I won't let you come for a week."

The door opened and two women walked in. Jazzie sat down hard on the chair Nathan had moved away from and tried to regain control. The conversations around her went unnoticed as she tried to figure out how to breathe again. He'd played her and she'd let him. She glanced over at him when she heard her name. Well, she thought, she would make him pay the next time they were alone. It would be worth whatever punishment he gave her just to take him down a peg or two.

Chapter 12

Tank moved along the side of the house to where the lady lived. He didn't like changes and this hit changed almost daily. The woman who'd hired him was a little off too, but he could live with that. Money made him overlook a great many weird things. He watched as the lights went out in the house behind him.

He was hot and itchy. He reached under the padding and scratched hard at the sweat rolling down his chest. Tank looked around again and decided that he could take off the cover up now, drop it here, and come back for it later. He pulled his shirt over his head and opened the Velcro as quietly as he could. Soon he had the thick rubber bodysuit off and the chilled night air was caressing his salty skin.

Tank was much smaller than Ginny thought he was. He knew what she was thinking; he'd heard it all before. She thought he was fat and lazy, disgusting, and a bit smelly. He'd added the smelly part by leaving his fat suit on for a few hours every day and not cleaning it up. It gave him more authenticity and besides, it made him laugh when people backed away from him.

But he liked having a disguise. No one came looking for him after a job was done. And he knew that they had. Most of the time when a job was finished the police would figure out who had hired him. Never him, but they certainly found their way back to the employer.

Tank took off his jogging pants and peeled out of the pants under them. He stood in the night air in just his boxers and allowed it to cool him down. He felt the hair on his body shimmer when a breeze moved along his skin while he was still damp. Twenty minutes later he was walking along the house again, this time a much smaller target than he had been.

The woman, Jasmine Waite, was home. He'd seen her come in over an hour ago. There was a male with her, but he didn't foresee a problem with him. Ginny had told him that he was a drunkard and a druggie and that he was more than likely sharing his drugs with the girl. Tank thought maybe she was wrong about that. In his experience druggies didn't share well.

A dog barked close. Tank tensed. There was very little he hated more than dogs and was afraid that one more thing had changed that he'd not been told about. The dog's barking grew fainter and he let go of the breath that he was holding.

He'd been doing a job up north when this little piss-ant of a dog had come out of nowhere and tore him up. The little fucker had bitten him so many times that he'd had to have stitches. He grinned. He'd hunted down the dog a few weeks later and killed him. A long and slow death that he was sure the dog had had a heart attack rather than die from any of the injuries he'd inflicted on him.

The door opening had him pressing against the house quickly. He'd been so busy thinking about the stupid mutt that he'd nearly been seen. He heard the voice of the girl then the man. He waited to see if what they were doing gave him a way to finish this job.

"What do you mean that's the way it goes? That's the fucking most... Come back here, you fucking ass, and explain this to me. I demand an answer." The girl had a mouth on her, that was for sure, Tank thought with a grin.

The man laughed and kept walking as he spoke over his shoulder. "You want me to come back then you'll do what I want. You know this is how it works and you'll learn to listen or you'll just have to suffer."

"You miserable excuse for a...I swear to Christ, I hate you." The man, Howard he thought he'd been told his name was, laughed again. "All right, but I'll have you know that I want a time when I can be bossy too."

The man came within touching distance of Tank as he walked back to the house. Howard paused for the briefest of seconds before he moved on. Tank held his breath, didn't move, and didn't even let his finger twitch.

When the door closed behind the couple Tank sank to the ground. His hands were shaking when he lifted them to rub over his face. That was as close as he'd ever been to being seen. At least being seen by anyone he didn't want to see him.

Tank stood up after several minutes. He was shot as far as taking out the girl and knew now that if he went into the house to finish them, he'd make a mistake. A mistake big enough that he'd be caught. Gathering up his suit, he walked and sometimes staggered back to his truck and sat in the cab for several minutes. When he felt as though he had some control he started the car and drove back to the house he'd rented. Nothing had ever made him feel so...exposed before.

He parked under the light that he'd broken out several days ago. He didn't like to bring attention to himself and a light where someone could watch him coming and going had had to go. Tank moved his things into the house, walked to the small bedroom in the back, and picked up the pictures of the girl.

He'd read the paper today about the girl and her being this famous writer. He'd not read any of her stuff, but had gone to the local bookstore to pick up one that they'd had on display. He'd been surprised about that, her being an author and all. The woman, Ginny, had made is sound as if the girl was just this side of retarded. He hated that word and didn't use it often, but he thought it apt. He compared the picture he had of her to the one in the paper.

She was pretty, though Tank was sure that most would think her beautiful. He didn't care for her looks himself. He preferred his woman to be on the plump side and a little homely. To his way of thinking they were more grateful about his inability to have a good erection unless he was cutting them and he thought they tended to stay with him longer. Though lately that theory was proving a bit on the wrong side. He sat at his little table and picked up the money.

He didn't need the money. He'd been a hired killer for nearly all his life. Tank had killed his first person at ten and had enjoyed it so much he'd killed four more people before he'd turned fifteen. But he'd known of Roscoe Waite and had heard the man had hated his kids. Plus, there was the fact that Roscoe had saved his daddy from being gang raped in prison and, in Tank's book, that made him an all right guy.

He looked at the newspaper again. Ginny had said she wanted the girl dead by next week. There was this book thing she was going to do on Monday afternoon so he tried to remember where the bookstore was. When he realized it was near the mall he decided that it would be the best time to do the job. Tank liked when things came together and he went to call Ginny. And he decided to try and convince her that she should sleep with him. Hell, he might even let her see the real him if she was as good as she looked. Chubby and sort of pretty with just enough age on her to make him want her bad enough to risk putting himself out there.

Tank went to his bathroom to jerk off. But that only ended up frustrating him. He couldn't stay hard long enough to make anything happen more than his hand getting sore and his dick hurting. He went to bed pissed off and not a little horny. He was finding a hooker first thing tomorrow when he got up. One less of those kind in the word wouldn't be missed.

~~~

Payton sat in the mall dining area and watched the people. He'd been sitting here for over three hours and hadn't moved much more than to go to one of the eating places and get a snack. He tended to nibble when he was nervous. And Payton was really nervous.

His wife Sin was expecting him an hour ago. And she wasn't happy. He knew this because she'd texted him five times in so many minutes. But he had a job to do and he had to finish it. When his assignment came toward him Payton sat up in his chair and glanced down at his phone when it vibrated again. He typed a single letter and slipped the phone into his pocket as he stood.

He was nearly out the door after his guy when he saw someone who he knew. Well, he thought, not really knew, but had seen recently. As recently as the wanted posters hanging in his office he shared with his brother-in-law McKee. He pulled out his phone again and made a call this time. Sin answered on the first ring.

"You'd better have a fucking good—"

"I see someone that could be connected to your family's problems." He heard her take a sharp breath. "I need you to go to the office and send me a pic of one of the men on the wall. I need to make a comparison. There is something that's just…something is different."

"Where are you? Do you need back-up?" He could hear her running as she spoke. "I can see Shamus' car in the drive. Let me send him to you." He told her to go ahead and where to find the picture he wanted. She said she'd have to take a picture of it with her phone and send it because she didn't have time to fuck with his fancy equipment.

He walked about fifty yards behind the man. He knew the face, just not a name he could put his finger on. Payton stepped into the candy shop as the man did and spoke to Sin again. "I know, honey," he said to her when the man stepped close. "But for now let me just get her a box of those chocolates. Yes," he continued in code. "You know the place in the mall, the one with the large cherry over the door?"

"All right. Shamus is leaving now. He said that you're old college buddies and you invite him to the bar. There is one at both ends of the place and you can go either way after the man."

"I think that'll be okay. Did you say white chocolate or was it that really weird kind?" He loved listening to her cuss at him. He had no idea why that turned him on so much.

"Fucking ass, will you just write this fucking shit down? I'm assuming a white male that looks weird. Weird how, you fucking ass? Does he have three eyes?"

He laughed. "No, just the normal amount. Remember the ones with designs on them. I love the small dragon ones, but I don't see one here."

"Dragon tat on his eye. Okay, can you tell me what color shirt he has on, smart ass?" Payton laughed again as the man purchased three pounds of dark chocolate and another five pounds of peanut butter fudge. He either had a very greedy girlfriend or the guy had some serious cravings.

"Dark chocolate," he said as the man walked by him and out the door. "He's on the move again. Do you know McKee's ETA? And by the way, very good on the code. I might make a detective out of you yet."

She snarled at him and he laughed as he slipped his Bluetooth in his ear and his phone in his top pocket. He watched his new target walk toward the bar and told Sin where to send McKee. The picture came through when he was talking to her and he hung up to look at it.

It was him, but it wasn't. The tattoo was new and the hair was different. It was a bit on the blurry side, but he was sure he was missing something. McKee sat down next to him and ordered a beer.

The two of them watched the man for several minutes. He didn't speak to anyone, only the waitress and then only to order another beer. He ate a piece of his candy and drank. When he got up and left the chocolate and a beer on the table to go to the bathroom, McKee stole his bottle and put it in his pocket. He was careful not to touch the lip as he slipped out of the busy bar. When the man returned there was a fresh beer in its place and nothing else was disturbed.

Payton snapped ten pictures of the man as he walked to the bathroom himself and another three when he walked by him to leave. He had no idea if any of them were going to be usable, but he'd tried.

He met his wife and his partner McKee in the parking lot. He kissed his partner on the cheek and shook hands with Sin. He knew that the likelihood of making McKee pissed enough to hit him for kissing him was slim, but Sin...? She told him she was going to murder him when she got him home. Life was grand as far as he was concerned.

"I asked a buddy of mine to run some DNA on the bottle. Might get a hit, but maybe not," McKee said after he'd threatened him with bodily harm. "What made you follow him anyway? The one that is paying us wanted you to follow someone else, I might add."

He took the picture Sin had brought with her and asked McKee to look at it and tell him what he saw. Payton had never met a more controlled mind than McKee's. The man was scary in the way he could break down a crime scene and even more scary when he was reading a report.

"Brothers? Nah, father and son maybe? He's been heavy at one time too," MrKee told them after a few minutes. "I'd say really heavy by the way he looks so...well, I was going to say loose, but he's more like one of those dogs with too much skin and not enough to fill it."

"Chinese Shar-Pei," Sin said without looking up from the file. "They are pretty loyal to their families. Very unlike the man you guys followed, or at least the one in the file is. His name is Michael Ross, also known as Major. He has a list as long as me. Says here that he died five years ago from AIDS. The man claimed he was...get this," Sin said, smiling as she looked up. "He was friendly with none other than Daddy Dearest in the state pen. According to this, Daddy Dear saved Major from a major butt-fucking—wonder if that's how he got his nom de plume."

Payton kissed her and took the file. She was having entirely too much fun and he wanted to be the hero. He started reading over the file when McKee's phone rang. He knew it was too soon for the test to come back so he sat on his car and read on. There was enough bad stuff in this file to have put the guy away for several lifetimes and couldn't understand why he'd been let out after ten years of a double life sentence.

They'd found every known associate to Roscoe Waite in prison and out. The man had made a great many enemies on the inside and even more when he'd gotten out. But the few that he had been loyal to had remained so even after Roscoe was killed. But Roscoe didn't have enough pull to get a guy out on...then he saw it. He looked over at McKee as he finished up his call.

"The fucking bastard got out because the star witness in his case suddenly had second thoughts and all the evidence from the case disappeared. It seems that someone had gotten into the lock up and destroyed it." Payton looked at his wife. "It claims that your mother was questioned."

Chapter 13

Jazzie walked in the bookstore she was supposed to be doing the signing in on Friday, three days from now. She immediately fell in love. It had the local business charm that she'd missed when she'd gone to the bigger stores, yet she could see that they had a great many of the best sellers she loved to read too. She was wandering through the section on cook books when someone approached her.

"Hello, are you finding everything you need? We have quite a selection of cook books in the do it yourself section too. Men don't like to shop in this area so we try to accommodate them."

Jazzie laughed. "No, I'm just…I'm Jazzie Waite. But I think you might know me as Jas—"

"Oh my, the author," she exclaimed as she took Jazzie's hand. "Oh my, oh my. I've been so looking forward to meeting you. And oh my, oh my, I read your book last night. All in one night too. Oh my, oh my."

Jazzie was charmed. She tried to pull her hand free, but the woman seemed to be pumping it for some other reason than Jazzie could fathom. When she finally released it, Jazzie put it behind her in the event that the woman said "oh my" again and reached for it.

She kept staring at Jazzie. Then she noticed the name badge. Mildred, it read, the woman she was supposed to meet within an hour. Jazzie smiled. She really liked this woman and her seemingly befuddled nature around her. "You're Mildred." The woman nodded. "You said to come by." Another nod. "I'm here."

"Oh my. Oh my, so you are. Yes, the meeting. You'll have to forgive me. I've only owned this shop for just over twenty-five years and you'd think I'd know better than to let a famous person...why don't we have a seat? I've got some seating places over here. The kids seem to like it. And oh my, the older generation seems to have the best time over here. And oh my, I love a good gossip session as much as the next."

They were no more than seated when a younger version of Mildred, including the occasional "oh my" joined them. The daughter, her badge claimed her to be Shelly, had read the book too.

"I couldn't put it down. And the steamy parts...oh my. I told Mother we'd have to put it in the paper about you being here and to tell the parents that you have a sensual twist to your books that might be a bit too much for the younger crowds." Shelly leaned forward and in a loud whisper said, "Though I think they have a better understanding of sex than some adults."

Jazzie agreed. She'd been aghast at what information she'd found on the Internet and even more so when she'd realized that a lot of her books were being bought by teenagers. But she knew that trying to control who bought her books would be like trying to control a fast moving river. She'd only frustrate herself and piss off her customers.

"I've never done a book signing before. Have either of you?" She didn't want them to be disappointed that no one showed up so she wanted to be honest with them. "I'm not sure if anyone will come to this. I've got some books out on the market, of course, and they sell well, but...well, I'm still trying to figure out why anyone buys them." She flushed when they both laughed.

"Honey, we've probably taken a thousand calls from all over the state wanting to know the times and if we will have enough books. We called that publisher of yours, Miss Midland? She set us up with a couple of vendors who said they'd help us out. I don't think you've gotta worry about anyone showing up. You should be more worried about having enough ink in your pen to sign them all." Mildred patted her on the knee as she continued. "You sure are a pretty thing too. Draw them men in like droves if we can put a picture of you in with the thing they are a running on Thursday."

Jazzie nodded her agreement and before she knew it she was posing with Mildred and Shelly and having a wonderful time. She only hoped she didn't look as nervous as she felt. She did make a note in her little book to maybe ask Drew or Chastity about having some pictures made that wouldn't have her looking like a dork.

She spent an enjoyable two hours with the women. She also got a great idea for another story. There was no way she was going to pass up the opportunity to use "oh my, oh my, oh my" in a book.

She went home feeling the best she had in a while. When she opened the garage door to pull in she frowned at the amount of boxes there and the sheer size of some of them. Just as she was getting out of her car a van pulled up.

"Miss Waite? We're with Bishop Equipment. Mr. Howard sent us by to set up his equipment." She looked at the boxes and noticed that they were covered in the name and logo of the local sports store. She pulled out her phone to call Nathan after asking the men to wait.

"It's a treadmill and a few other items I thought you could use. There are some men supposed to come by and set it up for you."

She was speechless as he continued. "So you thought I could use some gym equipment? I see." She waved the two men toward the boxes to take inside. She wasn't sure what she'd have them do with it once she got it in there, but she didn't think taking her hurt out on them would be very nice.

She realized that Nathan hadn't said anything. And she'd be damned if she would. At least not about him thinking she needed to exercise. So brushing at the tears that started to fall, she told him she had to go and hung up. He was saying her name when she closed the phone.

The men, Bob and Art, set the equipment up in her basement. She didn't even go down to see what all there was. But after telling them she was going to do some things in her office, she simply slipped out her back door and into the yard. She started walking toward her sister's house without any thought as to why. She was halfway there when she realized she'd left her cell phone in her purse, which was sitting on her table.

~~~

Nathan called her six more times before he decided to go to her house and find her. He was frantic when he got there and found not only was she gone, but the men had been sitting on her porch because the lady of the house had just disappeared.

"Said she was going to do some work, that we were to go about our business, but when we was finished, we couldn't find her. And we didn't want to leave her house all done open like this so we waited." Bob handed him the work order to sign. "You're a good customer, Mr. Howard, and we thought you'd want us to hang out."

He nodded and paid the men a generous tip. His mind was more on where the hell Jasmine could be and why the hell she hadn't let him explain about the equipment. He knew now that he should have explained before he'd bought it rather than think she'd understand after he had it set up.

They played. And when they played…well, there were times when they, especially he, was a little on the rough side. He didn't want her hurt and figured if she were to get used to the sometimes strenuous pulls on her muscles then they could play more. He'd never thought she'd think he thought she was fat. Alyssa had told him he'd be lucky if she spoke to him ever again.

"What the hell were you thinking? You buy a woman a treadmill and she immediately thinks you're saying she's fat. I know I would. Men," she said as she started pacing the room. "What did you buy her that for anyway?"

He wasn't going to tell her that he was into dark sex and that he didn't want to hurt Jasmine. He especially wasn't going to tell her that when he set up the kind of equipment he wanted to in Jasmine's basement he wanted to be able to tie her to the hump, bend her over, and fuck her tight ass.

"I thought we could work out together. She said she wanted to be in better shape and I wanted to surprise her." Which was all true.

"Oh you surprised her all right. You idiot." She picked up her phone. "You'd better have some major gifts for her when I find her. Otherwise you can kiss any makeup sex goodbye."

Two hours later Alyssa told him where he could find her. He thought maybe she knew sooner, but he didn't want to press. He was in enough trouble with the Waite women and had no desire to be castrated by any of them. Sin had been very descriptive about what she'd planned to do to him. Nathan was reasonably sure that some of the things she'd threatened him with might have been physically impossible. But on the other hand, knowing Sin, maybe not.

"She said she was visiting with Quinn and for you to go home. She said she'd be home in a bit and for you not to wait." Alyssa had told him she thought Jazzie was upset.

"She sounded like she'd been crying. But she kept saying she was fine when I asked her."

Nathan didn't understand women. He liked them. The way they moved, the way they smelled, especially after sex. He even liked to argue with one on occasion. And Jasmine could fight back with him really well. But he loved her and though she'd never said it back to him, he thought she loved him too. At least he hoped so.

He reached down and touched the small box in his pocket then at the one inside of his jacket. Both were still there. He hoped he wasn't doing more to piss her off, but he wanted her to know how much he loved her.

He pulled into Quinn and Drew's driveway and took a deep breath. He wanted a drink. That thought startled him into a sort of panic attack. He'd not thought of drugs or alcohol for nearly a year. He leaned his head on the steering wheel and started reciting the addict's Serenity prayer.

"God grant me the serenity to
accept the things I cannot change;
courage to change the things I can;
and wisdom to know the difference.
Living one day at a time;
enjoying one moment at a time;
accepting hardships as the pathway to peace;
taking, as He did, this sinful world
as it is, not as I would have it:
Trusting that He will make all things
right if I surrender to His Will;
that I may be reasonably happy in this life
and supremely happy with Him forever in the next. Amen"

He nearly said it again just for the strength it had always given him, but knew as surely as he was sitting there that the biggest strength he had was sitting inside the house in front of him thinking he'd insulted her. Taking another deep breath, Nathan went to face the music. He let out a long breath and knocked on the door.

Drew answered the door. His face said it all. "She's pissed at you no matter what she says. And for the record, I'm not so happy with you either. This is my date night with my wife and now she's in the other room with her sister and I'm getting nothing."

"I'm sorry. I never meant to hurt her. I need...do you think I could talk to her? It's important. And if she throws me out, I promise to go without a whimper."

Drew nodded and closed the door behind him. "They're in the living room. Quinn is ready to murder you too. And I understand that Sin is as well."

Drew looked happy and Nathan wanted to tell him he'd fucked up, to cut him some slack. But he was standing in the doorway and saw her.

He knew she was upset the moment he saw her. Her eyes were puffy and her nose was red. Nathan wanted to go to her and beg her to forgive him, but knew that she'd only tell him she was fine. Quinn got up and stood in front of him.

"She hurts, you hurt; you know that, don't you?" Nathan nodded, knowing she wasn't talking about his heart hurting like hers, but more physical. "Fix this."

He found himself in the room with Jazzie and was suddenly nervous. He moved toward the couch where she was sitting and sat in the chair across from her when she stiffened. He cleared his throat twice before he started to speak. She spoke first.

"I'm fine, really I am. I don't know what the big fuss is about. Why don't you just go home and I'll...you can call

123

me tomorrow." She smiled, but it didn't reach her eyes. "Nathan, I don't—"

"I love you." She looked away. "I'm sorry I hurt you. I never meant for you to think—no, don't speak," he told her when she looked back with her mouth open. "I never meant to hurt you. And I know I did."

She shifted on the couch. "Okay, you did. I guess I thought you...well, you know, enjoyed me. I didn't think you found me lacking in—"

"Lacking? Good Christ, woman, you nearly kill me every time we make love." He leaned back and adjusted his hard cock. "You have me so hard all the time that I'm barely getting any work done for thinking of you."

"But you bought that stuff, all that equipment. I thought that you were trying to say you wanted me to be in better shape. I thought that you thought I was...I don't know, fat."

He slid out of the chair and walked on his knees toward her. She opened her legs when he was close enough to touch her and he leaned in and kissed her gently on the mouth. She tasted warm and soft. He wanted her with him forever.

"I was trying to get you in better shape, but not like you think," he whispered against her mouth. "I want to be able to tie you to one of many toys and take you. I want you not to be hurt when I put you over a hump and beat your ass while I fuck that pretty ass of yours. You can't believe how much I want that."

She moaned as he slid his hand up under her blouse and flicked his thumb over her pert nipple. She moaned his name as he rolled it between his finger and thumb.

"I thought if we both used the equipment and toned muscles that we'd only use during play then you would enjoy it more." He lifted her blouse and bit at her nipple thought the bra. "I can see these with clamps on them. Tight with hot blood when I take them into my mouth. I want you to hang from a hanger from the ceiling and let me flog that pretty ass while you hold back."

"Nathan, please. My sister is probably standing there at the door ready to rescue me from you." She arched her back and filled his mouth with her breast.

"I want you to come home with me. I want to feel your pussy wrapped around my cock while I slide deep." He slid his free hand up under her skirt and between her thighs to her apex. "You're wet, baby. And so hot. I could probably slide you over my cock and be deep in seconds. The thought of you coming on me like that has me wanting to chance you screaming out and bring them both inside of here."

"Please. You have to stop."

He pulled his hand from between her thighs and he nearly moved back again when she moaned. "Jasmine, I need to ask you something. Something important. You know that I'd never hurt you, right?" He let out a breath he hadn't known he was holding when she nodded. "I love you, do you love me?"

"Yes. I think I have since…well, I think a small part of me loved you before I met you."

"Good." He grinned as he pulled out the smaller of the two boxes. "Then will you marry me?"

She did scream after all and brought not only Quinn and Drew, but Sin, Lilliane, Alyssa, Cain, and Payton too.

Chapter 14

Tank moved around the closed bookstore. There was very little in the way of security here, but he knew that could be a bad thing as much as a blessing. He looked for any devices in the windows that would indicate that they had something more than what he could see. He jerked back when he saw a movement out of the corner of his eye.

"Fuck," he said several times under his breath. He looked back in the window, more cautiously this time, and saw what he'd seen. Dogs, big fucking dogs too. He leaned back against the building and closed his eyes. This thing with killing this person was proving more troublesome than he'd been led to believe.

First, the woman he was targeted to kill wasn't stupid as the woman Ginny had said. She was extremely smart if her books were anything to go by. Then there was the fact that her own mother hadn't known about either the books or the lover. Tank frowned at the thought of the mother. There was something really weird going on with her too. She was just…well, he didn't know the technical term for whatever she was, but he was willing to bet that her kids didn't know either.

Then there was this thing with the book and the signing. Who didn't know that her own kid was this famous person that some big-wig television station was going to take and make a movie out of one of her books? Tank thought his own mother knew what he did for a living and was sort of happy about it. Not the killing part, but at how good he was.

Tank walked back to his car and got in. The clock on the dash said it was just after three in the morning. He tried to decide if he should go back to his shitty house or just nap there. He had a feeling that as soon as this hit was over, he needed to leave town in double time. He had already packed up most of his shit and had it in the truck with him. Tank leaned back in his seat and closed his eyes.

Ginny had been the one he'd been dealing with. He knew when he'd started talking with who he thought was her today that he'd been mistaken. It took him several minutes of conversation to realize that she, Guinevere he'd been told, didn't have a clue what the fuck was going on.

"You've been hired to kill Jasmine Zinnia, I understand that. What I don't understand is how you're supposed to do it." He had started to tell her what the other…well, what had been discussed, but she interrupted again. "I mean, you're huge. How on earth do you expect to get around quietly with all that fat on you?"

He wanted to sock her in the nose, but didn't. He simply stood there and stared at her trying to figure out what exactly was going on. He looked over at the mirror that seemed to take up a great deal of the one wall.

"I'm a professional. I do my job very well and I get results." He glared when she snorted. "I want to talk to the other person. I think you should do…do whatever you have to do to bring her around."

She looked at him as though she was afraid. Then she simply closed up. He saw her eyes seemed to glaze over then she raised her nose in the air. The transformation from confused woman to pissed off one was profound.

"I have no idea what you're talking about. You should know that I will discuss this with Ginny and when I tell her how you treated me, she will not be happy." She moved to the big mirror and started messing with her hair. "You should learn your place. And if I were you, I'd find one of those fat farms and try very hard to shed those three extra people you're carrying around."

When she'd walked away, he'd drawn his gun. He even had it pointed at her before he realized that he never left a job unfinished nor would he do so now. The woman was certifiable and as soon as he could, she was dead.

Tank drove back to the house. He wasn't sure what he was going to do here, but he knew that sleep was out of the question. It had been a long day, but he was just too wired to do any more than watch some of the porn movies that he'd gotten earlier that day. By the time he had watched three of them, he knew that he was going to have to go out and find himself some deadbeat hooker and do her. He fell asleep in the chair smiling for the first time since he'd agreed to do this shitty job.

~~~

Nathan moved into Jasmine's house that afternoon. He wasn't sure still whose idea it was, but he was glad for it. He thought maybe she wanted him there because she was nervous. He wanted to be there because he was as well.

He'd never considered marriage before. He knew what he'd have to deal with on a daily basis. He also knew what someone who wanted to spend a life time with him would have to do as well. It wouldn't be easy. It would be damned hard.

Being a recovering alcoholic was something that would be forever. He'd never not want a drink or something just to make things go better. The drugs would be the hardest to kick. They were just as easy to get, but the feelings that they gave him were more immediate. Plus, as far as he was concerned, they were much easier to hide from someone.

He knew because when he had been in one of the rehab places before his mother had died, he was high daily. The alcohol may have been taken away, but the cheap places his mother had shoved him into were not all that monitored and only wanted him there for the money he was bringing in. The last place he'd been in, the one his sister had put him in, was much stricter and much harder to get things by. He'd been caught so many times with something that he'd finally just given up and decided that he'd wait until he got out then get all he wanted.

But it hadn't worked that way. Once he'd been sober, and he meant really sober, he started to notice things. Smells for one thing. He could smell what they were having for a meal long before they announced it. Then there was the smell he got from his open window. He had been locked in his room because of something he could no longer remember and had opened the window to escape. He'd only managed to lean out and realized that he was seven stories up and a long way from just hopping out to escape.

It had been late June. The trees below him were a vivid green that made his eyes hurt, but the aroma that they'd given off had made him want to con one of the orderlies to bring him a handful of their leaves so that he could crush them in his hand and bring the scent to his nose. He'd felt foolish for thinking such a thought and hadn't said anything to anyone until he'd seen his therapist. She'd told him that he should have done it; it may have made him feel better. She was probably right. Smiling as he put the last of his CD's in with hers, he went into the kitchen to find Jasmine.

She was on the phone when he walked in. She was also in the process of cutting up some lettuce. He knew that she didn't like to cook and only did it when she didn't want to eat out. He also knew that while she didn't like it, she was very good at it. He took the knife from her and with a quick kiss to her nose, moved her to finish the job.

There was chicken on the stove in a pan. Along with the small chicken pieces, there were onions and peppers. In another pan was squash, carrots, and garlic. The smells made him realize that he'd not eaten since lunch that afternoon. He poured them both a glass of iced tea and half-listened while she spoke on the phone. He smiled when he realized she was trying to get out of whatever the person on the other end wanted her to do.

"No, I understand that there would be a great deal of exposure. But as I've said, I'm not ready to go on a—of course I know who she is. I'd have to be dead not to, now wouldn't I? I'm just saying that I'm not comfortable with— if you interrupt me one more time before I finish a sentence, I will call my attorney."

He looked up when she snorted. He had to hand it to her, she could make a man listen when she used that tone. He grinned when she started talking again. It sounded like the person on the other end of the line believed her too.

"Now, as I was saying, I'm not very comfortable with going on a television circuit just yet. I've only just released that I'm Jasmine Blackwell. I'd appreciate it if you'd just give me a few more weeks to get used to all the attention." She took out a pad of paper he knew she was never without. "I will make note of that now and let you know. If you'll call my…secretary and let her know what dates are available then I'll see what I can work out." She gave him the phone number that Drew had helped her set up today. After she hung up, she sat in the chair and stared at the glass in front of her.

"I can probably delay this if you want. It smells really good, but if you need to just unwind then we can start over on something else if this isn't fit to eat later." She looked up at him when he spoke. He wasn't sure she heard him.

"I don't think I can do this. I don't think I can be this person these people think I am and be sane too. It's too…it's too much."

He walked around the big bar and took her hand when he sat next to her. "What is it you think they want from you, honey? And just so you know, I'm very proud of you."

"Proud? I don't know why. I'm sort of overwhelmed that… That person wanted me to come onto a daytime show and tell them all about my life and how it made me into a writer. I can't tell them that I became a writer because in order to escape my childhood, I dreamed up these people and pulled them out when I was lonely or scared. They'll think I'm insane."

He picked her up and pulled her into his lap. He held her for several minutes as the warmth of home surrounded them. He knew in that moment that he could never love anyone as much as he did this small woman in his arms.

"I think they'll think you're brave and smart. You dealt with something that would have hurt a weaker child. Look at what I did to deal. I turned to drugs and drink." She started to speak, so he kissed her to quiet her. "You're not to tell me that what we had was different. We are the same when it comes to our childhoods. The only difference is that I dealt with it by hiding and you with words."

"But didn't we both hide?" she asked him quietly.

Had they? Yes, she was probably right, but her way made her a much stronger person and, in turn, would do the same for him. He kissed her again and told her that he loved her. "And if you don't feed me soon I'm going to have to resort to nibbling on you." He nipped at her shoulder. "While the chicken might be better for me in the long run, I'm thinking you might be the best thing I've ever tasted."

They finished cooking the meal together then worked on cleaning up the kitchen. There were things, things only she would understand, that he told her while they ate. He told her things that he'd not been able to tell his therapist. Then he shared with her the first time he'd tried to kill himself. Well, the first time he'd attempted to kill himself that didn't involve him getting high every day.

"I'd been about eighteen. My drug consumption was through the roof and I was spending, on average, about ten grand a week. My dad…well, Alyssa's dad had just died. He was the only one…well, he was the only male that had ever given any kind of straight talk to me. My uncle Samuel, who turned out to be my real father, had only been my supplier."

"Oh God, Nathan, I'd forgotten about that. Alyssa told us right after she married my brother all about…" He turned his back to her and waited.

"Yeah," he said when she didn't go on. "I knew about that. It was something I'll be ashamed of for the rest of my life. I was just sober enough to know what they were doing, but could only hang onto my own misery about losing the only man who'd tried to make a difference in my life. Right after Alyssa disappeared…I found myself in the garage. I'd been at a party and I couldn't…Christ, this isn't easy."

She wrapped her arms around his waist from behind and held him. He put his hands over her and closed his eyes. He had to tell her if for no other reason than he needed her to understand.

"Nathan and Alyssa had been close. I think maybe he'd known for some time that we, my brother and I, weren't his children. He never treated us any differently. In fact, I was hard pressed to think it was true, but the blood work, even the one my mother had a doctor try to fix, told it all. We were not his sons. But him leaving the money to Alyssa, all of it, was the smartest thing he could have done. We'd have gone through it in no time and still it wouldn't have been enough." They moved to the living room as he continued.

"I'd heard them talking, Uncle Samuel and Mom. They had this idea that if Alyssa got pregnant by Samuel, they'd

133

get more money to raise it. And then of course they'd have to have her declared unfit and then have her committed to watch over the money and the kid. I don't think they thought she'd go along, so they..." He got up and started pacing. "They asked me the best drug to give her to incapacitate her." He didn't look at her. He just continued pacing the floor. He'd already told Alyssa. He'd told her the first day he'd gotten out of rehab. She'd been so quiet that he was sure she'd never forgive him, but she simply got up and wrapped her arms around him and told him she was sorry.

"I asked her why she was sorry," he told Jasmine. "I asked her what on earth she had to be sorry for when it was me who had basically given her the drugs to make her sick enough that they could try. And do you know what she said? She said, 'but you didn't, and that I was just as much a victim as she was."

"And you were," Jasmine told him softly. "Maybe more so. You had to live with what they'd done and she...she escaped the only way she knew how. I can't imagine that either one of you had a lot of choice in what happened and both of you, you as much as Alyssa, has overcome so much to be the people that you are now. The people I love."

He made love to her slowly that night. Not because he thought she needed it, but because he did. He needed that soft connection to her, to someone who loved him. He entered her slowly, his cock filling her and completing him. Then he held himself still above her as he looked down at her.

"I love you, Jasmine Waite. I will love you for longer years than there are stars in the sky. And I want us to have children together. I want to see you swollen with our child, feel you move with one. Will you, darling? Will you have a baby with me?"

"Oh Nathan, there is nothing in this world I'd want more."

His release was mind-blowing. He came inside of her deep and knew that, if nothing else, this woman completed him in way that he'd never be able to find with anyone else.

Chapter 15

The bookstore was packed. Jazzie could hardly move without bumping into someone. She tried to make her way to the door to…well, escape came to mind, but there was someone always wanting to ask her something. When someone took her hand, she nearly screamed she was so terrified. She turned to look at Alyssa.

"You look ready to bolt. I wouldn't if I were you. You might cause a riot. Take some deep breaths." Jazzie nodded at her. "Nathan said you asked him not to come down."

"I was afraid no one would show up and I didn't want him to feel sorry for me. I wish now I hadn't been so hasty. Oh God, Alyssa, these people are here to see Jasmine Blackwell, not me." She felt herself start to panic again. "I need to leave. Right now, I need to leave."

"No, you're not. Calm down." Alyssa put her arm around her and pulled her in for a quick hug. "You're going to be fine. And you are Jasmine Blackwell, you dork. You have half an hour before you start signing books and I think we should take a stroll around the street. Look, there's Quinn and Sin now."

Jazzie looked up to see her other two sisters. Lilliane joined them a few minutes later. Gracie had sent her three dozen red roses and the sexiest under things she'd ever seen. She'd told her to wear them under her clothes and only she'd know how incredible she looked in them. Well, her and the man who'd answered the phone. She wouldn't be able to make it to this one, but when she came to New York for a signing, she'd throw her a bash of all parties and they'd celebrate in style.

They walked out of the bookstore together after telling Mildred they'd be back. After reassurances from the book store owner they began to window shop down the street. Sin snorted when Jazzie reminded them that their mother's birthday was day after tomorrow.

"She should be giving us gifts instead of us giving her anything," she said. "The old bitch needs to be smacked for what she said to Lilly Pad."

Sin had never been one to forgive and forget. Not, at least, when it concerned their mother. And Sin hated their father. She'd drawn a gun on him once when he'd threatened to beat her ass after she'd come home for a visit. Jazzie went out and learned how to fire a weapon right after her sister had left and had become quite the marksman—or woman.

"I think I'm going to get that for Nathan, though," Jazzie said as she stared at the watch in the jewelry store display. "I know that the one he uses now keeps miserable time and I want to give him something." She glanced at the other women in the reflection of the glass and saw the man behind them. He looked out of place and she started to turn when Sin told her no.

"He's from the bookstore. Don't acknowledge him in any way. And please don't act nervous." Sin touched her waist and Jazzie knew she was armed. "He won't get to you. I swear, he won't get to any of us if that is his plan."

Jazzie went inside the jewelry store and bought the watch. The person was going to engrave it, but it would take a few days. While they were inside Sin told her quietly what they thought was going on. And that Payton and Shamus were watching as well.

138

"His dad and ours were in prison together. So far, we can't make a connection to him and Roscoe, but we aren't going to take any chances. He's been around for about a month now. Not really doing much, but he has been seen around town." Sin picked up a small bracelet and purchased it for Tonya. "They, the police, think maybe he's a crazed fan."

"But you guys don't think so, do you?" Jazzie asked her. "Then what do you think he wants?"

"You." They headed out the door and back to the bookstore. "You could be the next target in this whole fucked up thing going on with our family. I don't want to believe that someone would continue to hurt one of us, but there are too many…way too many things pointed to us being on someone's hit list."

Jazzie found herself sitting at a long table with hundreds of people lined up to buy her book before she could sort through what her sister said. Sin had been happy to know that Jazzie was armed and that she carried her weapon all the time, but she hadn't been thrilled when she told her that she couldn't shoot someone to kill them.

"And do you think if he gets the opportunity he'll just let you go?" Sin practically snarled at her quietly. "No. He'll blow your fucking head off in a heartbeat."

So she tried to make small talk to each person who brought her the book and listened when they told her why they loved her. Most of the people were just amazed that she was so "normal," a few called her. While a few more told her that she inspired them to write, themselves, and if she would mind reading what they had. She directed those people to her publisher, telling them gently that she had no time to read anymore that she was trying to finish up the next series.

Jazzie hoped that the next time her publisher pushed her into something like this she'd remember that she could fight dirty too. She smiled when Nathan came in with Cain, Shamus, and Payton. Each of them purchased a book and she wrote something more in Nathan's. He flushed when Cain asked to read it. She was still laughing when the man from outside set his book in front of her.

"Make it to my mom. Her name is Bettina, Bettina Marshall."

She opened the book to the first page and picked up her pen. She was slightly nervous and was really surprised when Sin handed her a bottle of water.

Just as she was about to tell her no, she didn't want it, somehow the bottle slipped from her fingers and before she or Sin could catch it, the thing went flying. Before she could stand and mop up the mess, Sin was snatching the book away and had paper towels right there. Within seconds the book was gone, the water was cleaned up, and a fresh book was in front of her. She looked up at the man again.

"My sister is a little clumsy. She seems to get worse all the time." He laughed at her a little nervously and she opened the book again, careful of any bottles and of her sister, who was nowhere to be seen. "If you'll give me your address, Mr. Marshall, I'll make sure that your mother gets the next copy for free because of this. I don't want fans to think we're all bumbling idiots."

He told her not to worry about it and took the book almost as soon as she closed it. He nearly knocked down two women on his way out. Jazzie tried to make a joke about him being embarrassed and the women around her laughed. She wanted to find her sister and beat the snot out of her, but didn't get the chance. She spent the next four hours signing books and talking with "fans."

~~~

Tank got out of there fast. He knew what had happened in there even if the girl signing his book hadn't. The sister had gotten his prints. And as sweaty as he'd been around all

140

those people, he would bet she got his DNA too. Fuck, and double fuck.

He had to think, so he pulled in an alley and turned off his engine. He'd been so scared that he'd not even made sure he wasn't being followed. He watched the traffic flow behind him and didn't see anyone who seemed to be going slow, so he relaxed a bit, but not entirely.

He'd known that the girl was some kind of cop. He'd never really understood the woman when they'd described that one, but only that she was something in the army and that she'd been a failed attempt too. Tank wondered who the fuck these people were that they hung out with cops, rich broads, and writers. Of course they knew they were family, but what kind of family hung out in packs like these did?

He looked over at the book and thought about tossing it in the dumpster, but decided that he'd use it as a souvenir when this was over. He picked it up and began reading the first page. He was into the fifth chapter when he realized it was late and he could go troll the streets again for a woman.

Tank started in the lower east side. He wanted the right kind of woman, not just a hooker. He wanted one that was plump and a little on the lower side of thirty. Someone that he could fuck if he wanted and, when he was finished with her, no one would miss her. He thought he'd found the right one twice, but someone else would pull up and she'd get in the car with them. Just when he was ready to give up she walked out onto the street and he knew he had to have her.

Her hair was long and dark. He thought maybe it was red, but under the lights she was standing, it was just hard to tell. She looked to be about thirty-five, maybe a little older, but not much. She also looked to be about twenty pounds overweight. He pulled up along the curb just as she was leaning against the stop sign.

"Need a date, big boy," she purred into his open window. "Or are you out cruising? I can show you the best places to ride on if you have the cash."

He knew the code. She'd do him in the car and she knew the perfect place to do it without getting the cops busting them up. Tank didn't speak, but opened the automatic locks for her and she climbed inside. After a quick exchange of money they were on their way. She picked up his book off the seat.

"Hey, I read about her today. Says she is gonna be making a movie on the hobo station. Mary said that the books got the most wonderful sex scenes in 'em." She looked over at him. "That what you wanna do, lover boy? Something you read in this here book? I'm game if'n you are."

"Yeah," he told her. "I'm wanting to do what she and her lover do on page seventy. You look it up while I drive." He was glad now that he'd not thrown the book out and that he'd read some of it. Who would have thought that a book would get him laid? He reached down to the side of his seat and felt the knife he'd just bought today. It was sharpened to a razor cut and he had a hard-on just thinking about plowing it into her. Or course, this was after he played with her for a while.

She directed him to an alley just off the middle of nowhere. He parked where she'd said and pointed out that the lights down this way had been knocked out by her pimp some years ago and nobody had gone in to replace them.

"Budget cuts," she told him. "That and the mayor taking a major cut to supply his mistress. Hell, there ain't much left for a couple of light bulbs on a dead end street."

As soon as the engine was off she leaned over and unzipped his jeans. His cock was hard, stone hard, and when she released him from his boxers he heard her sharp intake. He leaned back when she took him into her mouth.

He picked up the knife and was running it along her back when she nipped at his full head. He moaned, knowing that when he cut her, she was going to bite him harder. He put his free hand on the back of her head and pumped her up and down his cock while he cut her bra open.

Before she could lift her head up to protest, he cut her. Her scream was loud and he could feel her teeth sinking into his cock. *Yes*, his mind screamed. He ran the knife along her spine, deep enough to draw blood, but not enough to end what they were doing. She was struggling now. Her head was coming up so far off his cock that he knew if he hadn't held her there, she'd lose him. As he pounded her head up and down his dick, he cut her again and again. Blood poured from her and onto the seat beneath them. He was glad now that he'd taken the precaution to cover the seat with a sheet of plastic then a blanket he'd picked up at Goodwill.

He was close, so close that when he felt her bite him again, he shot his load deep into her throat. Her gagging only made him come harder. As the last of his cum spilled from his cock, he buried the knife into her back and straight through her heart. She dropped on him as he jerked twice more.

Tank sat there with the dead woman on his lap. He felt relieved, sated too. He lifted her head off his lap and moved her to the seat. His cock was covered in blood, some his and some hers. He wrapped his fist around his still hard shaft and used the blood to jerk off. He'd never done this before and the sensation was amazing. Her warm blood along his hot dick made him come quickly. Cum shot up out of him and all over the steering wheel and the dash as he shouted out his release. Tank laid his head back against the seat and smiled.

He knew he needed to get rid of her body, but he wanted to enjoy the soft afterglow of coming so nicely. He knew that once he finished up with the hooker, he was going back to the house and sleeping like a baby.

Tank got out of the truck and walked around while he stripped off his clothes. He pulled his duffle out of the back, as well as the large trash bag. He found himself whistling while he cleaned himself up. Three gallons of water poured over his head as he soaped himself off. As soon as he was fairly clean, he went to the other door and pulled the body out.

He dumped the three gallons of bleach he brought with him all over her. He did this naked so he was very careful to keep the chemical from his body. Once he had her covered in the stuff he dumped another gallon of laundry detergent on her. After wrapping her up in the plastic from the seat, he took her over to the dumpster just behind him and tossed her in it. He knew it would be days before they found her and maybe, if he was really lucky, they would never find her. After pouring the last two gallons of water over his head again, he pulled out the cheap towel and dried off. By the time he was dressed again, he was getting tired. He drove back to the house, crawled into his crappy bed, and fell asleep immediately. He didn't even bother setting his alarm, just simply tossed it onto the dresser.

His room was bright with light when he woke. It took him several seconds to try and sort through the noise coming from somewhere deep in his sleep. He finally sat up and looked around and realized that his cell phone was chirping. He got up and barked hello into it when he got it opened.

"I want to know why you didn't do what you said you were going to do yesterday." He tried to remember what he was supposed to do when she spoke again. "The fucking girl, you bastard."

For a minute, he thought she was talking about the hooker. That was the only woman he'd killed yesterday and had a fleeting moment of wondering how the hell she'd found out. And who the fuck was this anyway? He started to ask when he remembered.

144

"You fucking telling me how to do my job, bitch? It's too fucking early in the morning for you to be bitching about how I do what I do best. She'll get dead, you just keep your panties on. Unless, of course, you wanna go down on me. I got a hard-on that'll even impress you." His cock immediately hardened at the thought of killing this bitch. "Come on over. Let me show you how I like it."

Her laughter grated along his nerves. He felt his fist tighten around the phone and he wanted to crush it like he did her head. This woman was going to have to pay for this. She was entirely too uppity for his tastes.

"It's three in the afternoon, you moronic jackass. What did you do, find some hooker and get your rocks off in some dark alley?" He froze at her comment. "You'll start doing things my way or so help me, I'll find someone who will. I'm tired of fucking with you. I want her gone. Today."

Tank closed the phone and sat on the bed. There was something wrong here. He wondered when he'd lost control of the situation and the way things were going. Then there was the woman. He'd known from the start that she wasn't right. He also knew that he had to either finish this now or leave. He decided that if he didn't finish it today then he was leaving. There were strange things going down and he didn't want to be a part of it.

Chapter 16

McKee looked around the dump area. The woman in the dumpster had been dead for less than twelve hours. What the person had done to her would be forever burned in his memory. He looked up when he heard his name. Captain Grant came toward him and she didn't look happy to see him.

"Howdy, Capt. Nice morning, wouldn't you say?" He stood up and towered over her. But for reasons he couldn't explain she still made him feel small. "I think it's going to be a hot—"

"Don't even try that good ol' boy shit on me, McKee. What the fuck are you doing at my crime scene? You don't work for me last time I looked." She glanced around the area and her men. In a lower voice, she asked him what he knew she would. "Does this have anything to do with your family?"

He nodded. "We put a tracker in one of the books that Jazz signed yesterday. The guy had been on our radar for a couple of days. And before you get all huffy, let me finish." He smiled when she snorted. "We had nothing on him. Not even a name until this morning. Sin pulled some fancy moves and got the tracker on him and his prints all in one. We even got a nice bit of his sample too. Seems his profile has been in a few murders around the state and no one had anything to go on. Now we have a picture to go with a bit more."

He handed her the printout they'd gotten this morning. McKee didn't know who Alyssa knew in the lab, but they'd gotten these results faster than the feds would have. He so loved being a private dick with lots of toys to catch the bad guys. He looked around the site again as Cait read over the report. He noticed something shiny just under the dumpster.

He was fishing it out when Cait came up behind him. "You found this girl because of the tracking device, right?" He said yes. "Then tell me how that led you to the girl."

"It was in the book, which we found wrapped up in the plastic. And this wasn't just a spur of the moment kind of killing, Capt. He brought stuff to hide the evidence. Her body was covered in bleach and laundry detergents. And from the soap residue we found around this area I would say that he cleaned himself up here as well."

He pulled the knife free. It might have been from something else and not with this crime scene, but he had a hunch. He turned on his heel to look at Cait with the knife pinched between his finger and thumb. She immediately called for an evidence baggie. He looked at the knife as they waited.

It was a nice one and sharpened to a fine hone. He figured that it would cost in the neighborhood of around five hundred bucks at one of the shops on Richardson. He looked up at Cait when she whistled.

"I've seen that before. Not that one maybe, but one like it. Its army issue. Top of the line, usually carried by some of the darker forces they have. Might want to run it by Sin. I'm betting she can even tell you what tour it's from." She handed him a Clorox wipe as she continued. "This guy, you have a name for him yet?"

"Just a few aliases. I'm thinking I'll call Sin and see if she's busy. I know she was out on an assignment this morning and she's probably biting at the chain they have her on right now." McKee grinned before he told her why. "She was…she said she fell. Thing is, I don't think I've ever seen her fall unless she was falling on top of Payton. Just between us, he told me she was shot. Girl is a walking danger zone."

McKee laughed out loud when Cait started cussing. He was glad to see someone else get upset over it. Payton was a really laid back guy except when it came to his wife and daughter. The man nearly came unglued when the call had come through that she'd been hurt. And he wasn't so sure he'd be any different if it had been his wife. Lilliane was the world to him and he was really looking forward to his child coming any day now.

"Damned girl. She needs to have her ass beaten. I swear…" She looked up at him when he laughed again. "This is so not like me in the line of duty. I wear a vest. She, on the other hand, is out there in those skinny clothes making men drool then shoot at her."

"Yeah, but she's fucking good at it." He led her over to the body that they had covered up. He looked up at her. "You ready for this? The bleach did a number on her skin and, well…I think maybe he poured some down her throat. I'm thinking maybe she might have gone down on him and he came in her mouth. Seems a bit of an overkill when he left her belly full."

"Not if she didn't have time to swallow." He pulled back the tarp and Cait leaned down. "How many wounds and what killed her, do you know?"

"Seventeen, and it looks like he got her straight through the heart. The others, the ones on her back, look to me like she was lying down. If they were in his vehicle then maybe she was laying over his lap giving it to him and he tortured her while she was doing it. She had to fucking hurt. I asked around and this hooker is only into straight shit. Her name is…" He pulled his notepad out of his pocket. "Damsel.

Thinking that's a fun name, I had somebody run it for me. She's Roslyn Stafford from Cincinnati. She was thirty-six with a few priors of prostitution and a couple petty shoplifting. She had a small drug bust about four years ago, but nothing major. Her pimp, get this, is our boy Donny Newton. Questioned him and he has an air tight. Too bad, I really hate that guy."

Newton was a small time hustler and big time prick. He didn't treat his girls too badly, but he did run a harem of them. McKee had had a couple of run-ins with him in the past few months, mostly about some fights he'd had when one of the customers had an issue. He was sure that Cait had the same problems.

"Let's get her loaded. Then I want you to give me all you have on this scene. I'm not going to even ask you to fudge your knowledge of how you found her. Let's just put it down as you were a concerned citizen and not a fucking dick."

Shamus grinned. "You wound me, Capt. I am concerned citizen. And I was just walking by the area when this…smell came from this area and I thought I'd look around." She snorted again. "You know, I've never known you to be a skeptic."

The body was loaded into the van and she and McKee looked around the area again. He was glad she was there. It made his job easier because she was one hell of a cop. They talked about the case and the way their family was being targeted. He told her that they were taking every precaution with the other two, including Grace, who told the family she was not coming home.

"I don't know Grace well. She was always so quiet when they came around. And when she moved away when she turned seventeen no one really blamed her," Cait said as she walked him to his car. "There was always something so wounded about her. Like she has this major secret that she is terrified to tell anyone, or to let anyone get close enough to her to help."

McKee agreed. He had only seen Gracie, as they all called her, a few times. Mostly, it was over a quick weekend at one of the weddings, but she called Jazzie the most. He slipped another file to Cait that he pulled from his car.

"Payton and I wanted you to see this. It might not be anything, but then again…" He watched her look the file over. "We don't have anything solid on any of those men, but we do have enough to know that they were known to Roscoe. I know he's dead, but someone is pulling the strings. What we don't know could fill a fucking book. But that information could lead us a bit closer to *who*. I'm thinking that as soon as we figure out the 'why,' the 'who' might be a bit easier."

McKee took a picture of the knife then sent it to Sin. She said she was in the middle of something right now, but would get back to him. He figured she was probably begging either Payton or her commanding officer to let her go back to work and he hoped to hell neither of them gave in. He grinned. He might just let it slip to her brother that she was hurt. He could bring her to heel faster than anyone.

McKee decided to make another stop. He was just going into the flower shop when his phone went off again. He answered with a frown. He didn't get calls from Nathan all that often and was sure this wasn't going to be good.

~~~

Jazzie watched the police pull up. She wasn't at all surprised to see Cait Grant slip out and McKee to pull up behind the police captain. She was surprised to see her brother and Lilliane pull in. She wondered where Sin was, but didn't get a chance to ask when she was suddenly being hugged to death. Cain could hug like it was his mission. She turned and glared at Nathan again. He just couldn't let it go.

Someone had broken in. Not only had they broken in, but they had destroyed the place. Everything she had, including the food in the refrigerator, had been tossed around. There was a jar of mayo that was even spread over the couch in the living room and her bathroom had been...she wasn't sure what they had thrown all over in there, but if the smell was any indication it was shit. She was more pissed than scared. The only room that hadn't been messed up was her office. And it wasn't for lack of trying.

She'd gotten into the habit of locking her office door when she'd lived in the apartment and she hadn't gotten out of it. She looked again at the mess on the lawn and thought about all the work that would have been lost if they'd gotten in there.

The door had been pried on. The jamb around it had so many gouges that it looked like someone had used a chainsaw on it. Jazzie was glad now that she'd put in the reinforced steel doors and had had the windows throughout the house barred. Cait came at her with what she'd always assumed was her take-no-prisoners look.

"You all right?" Jazzie nodded and, before she could tell her that she was fine, Cait continued. "Have you touched anything? Or noticed anything that's missing?"

"No, I don't know. It's a mess. I'm sure...they didn't get into my office, but the door will need to be replaced and I'll have to paint again. I hate painting." Cait looked at her funny. "I'm nervous, so sue me. I babble when I'm nervous."

Nathan put his arms around her and pulled her into his embrace. She leaned back against him, but was no less pissed about what he'd done. She'd told him to forget it, nothing was taken that she could see and they were both all right.

"We weren't home. When we got back today we saw that the front door was open and called Shamus and Payton. I'm assuming one of them called you," Nathan said softly.

"McKee. He was with me not five minutes before he got the call. I was just around the corner when he called me to tell me there had been a break in." Cait looked up when someone said her name. "They cleared the house, so if you wouldn't mind going through it with one of my officers, we'll see what they might have taken."

Jazzie told her she'd already been through it when Nathan told her there was no one there. "Nothing's gone that I can see. Whoever it was…Cait, they tore up everything, even my food." She took several deep breaths. She didn't want to cry and she wouldn't. Not now, at any rate. She started for the door when Cait stopped her. She was looking at the door.

"They didn't break in. Does anyone besides you and Nathan have a key to this place?" Jazzie shook her head, but before she could say that the door was messed up too Cait continued. "See the glass? It's broken outside the house, not in. Which means that they were in the house before they broke the glass to make it look this way. Whoever broke into your house either had a key or they are good at picking locks."

Jazzie knew little about crime scenes, but she had the beginnings of a major story brewing in her mind as she walked behind Cait and noted all the damage. The rooms took on a more surreal look this time. She had decided to look at this from a reader's point of view rather than hers. It made it easier for one thing, and for another she could see things the way she described them. Sort of like she'd opened a blank page and was taking it all in to tell her readers about it.

"The walls had been gouged with something sharp," she started. "The carpet is covered in everything imaginable, including things I'm sure that I don't want to think about. The upholstery has been cut on all the furniture and all the stuffing pulled out of not only the cushions, but the back and arms too. The music collection was extensive, about three hundred together, and every one of the cases has been broken and all the discs are shattered. The television is broken. I think...did they throw a plant through it? Who throws plants through televisions?" She wasn't really looking for an answer, just babbling again, but Nathan answered her anyway.

"Sick people. They even broke the remote. I guess we'd have to replace the television anyway. It's easier than trying to reprogram one of those suckers." He picked the plant out of the screen and set it on the floor. "I think we can save this one."

She smiled at him. He was trying to be humorous and, while it didn't work, she did appreciate it. This was too much. She looked around again, then at Cait. She could no longer fight the tears.

"I can't stay here now. I have to...why did they do this? I've never done anything to anyone that would warrant this much...this much meanness." She didn't manage to catch the sob that spilled from her lips. "I need to go, please. If you need anything else would you mind asking Nathan?"

Without waiting for an answer she bolted from the room and the house. She'd sell it now. She'd have to. She no longer felt like she was safe there. It would be tainted, thanks to that person. She was nearly to the car again when someone grabbed her from behind. She started to struggle, but heard Nathan tell her it was him and she sagged against him.

"Shush now," he told her. "There isn't anything in there that we can't replace. In fact, maybe this is the perfect time for us to get us something together. It'll be fun picking out furniture and stuff. Or we can build. Something just our own. What do you think?"

She looked up at him. "I'm so sorry about your things. I didn't mean for anything to…they did this because they want me dead. Want me dead like they did my sisters. Why, Nathan? What did I do to them?"

"Nothing, honey. Nothing at all. And I'm not worried about some stupid things. I've got you and that's all that matters to me." He held her tighter when Cain walked toward them. Stalked would have been a better term.

"If you argue with me, I'm going to beat your ass. You are moving in with Alyssa and me until this is over. And if you think I'm going to take no for an—"

"I'll take care of her, Cain," Nathan said in a low voice. "She's mine now and I'll take care of her. While we appreciate the offer, we'll be looking for something to build. I'm not sure where we'll be staying, but I assure you that we'll be well secured."

Cain looked like he wanted to argue, but didn't. He finally nodded as if he'd come to the conclusion it would do him no good. He smiled slightly before he spoke. "Okay. But if you wouldn't mind staying with us, Alyssa and I would love to have you both. We have plenty of room and…fuck it. Please, I'll feel so much better if you'd move in with us. I know you have her, but she's still my little sister."

Nathan looked down at her. She nodded slightly and he turned back to Cain. To be honest, she thought maybe she'd enjoy living there for a bit. She was terrified out of her mind, if truth be known. Nathan told Cain they would, but only temporarily. Cain seemed to relax a bit.

They all decided to go back to Cain's for dinner as the police finished up. Nathan and Cain, with the help of a couple of police and Shamus, gathered up all her things from the office she was afraid to leave and took them to the car. She was just getting inside when her cell phone rang.

The unknown scared her. When Lilliane had gotten calls last year from someone out to get Shamus, that was how they'd contacted her. She looked up at Nathan.

"Don't answer it. If it's anything important, they'll leave a message or not. Whatever they have to say, you're safe with me." Nathan held her while the ringing continued. When the sound for a message rang she handed the phone to Shamus with her code.

He listened and then grinned. "It's your editor. She has book seven finished for you, but has a question about one of the scenes. She wants you to call her back on the name of the condom you used. She said she thinks maybe she's used it before and if your facts are true, which she doesn't doubt, she's going to kill her boyfriend."

Flushing, Jazzie took the phone back. "You should know that I never work without all the facts." She flushed again when he asked her what they were using. She decided that she didn't much care for Shamus at the moment and slipped inside the car and slammed the door. She could still hear his laughter as he walked away.

She leaned back in the seat as Nathan drove them over to Cain and Alyssa's house. She was just thinking up ways to get back at Shamus when she dozed off. She didn't even realize she'd fallen asleep until Nathan woke her up after they stopped.

Chapter 17

Ginny paced her room. She just knew that stupid bastard had killed that woman who was all over the paper and news today. Found body, it had said, mutilated and dead. She wanted to toss something at the screen, but didn't want to miss if they said anything about having any suspects. So far all that cunt of a police captain said was that they were looking at all avenues at this point and would find her killer.

Killer. The fucking bitch was a prostitute. What the fuck did she think was going to happen if she walked the streets for money? That someone was going to invite her home for tea and crumpets? Maybe invite her into their home and make her their honorary aunt or something? Ginny picked up the book that was lying on her bedside and threw it at the wall. Fucking bitch.

She glanced over at the screen in time to see Cain. She hurried to the remote and froze the screen. There was her man. Cain Waite was hers and she couldn't wait to get him between her thighs. She nearly moaned when she reached between her legs and felt her cream gathering there. She went to her bed and reached for her vibrator. The thing would get her off but not satisfy her, but with Cain so close like this she was sure she'd really enjoy herself.

Ginny pulled her pants and panties off. She had the purple rabbit up inside of her before she'd even turned it on.

By the time the tiny ears were touching her clit she was riding it hard. She imagined Cain there, his tongue deep inside of her as he tasted her. She started pushing the hard shaft against her clit and crying out every time it touched her. She was so close to coming that she knew that when she did finally have him she wouldn't be able to stop with just a one-time fuck. She'd have him tied up for a month. She looked up at the frozen screen to see his mouth curved up and thought of his cock fucking her when she came with a scream. Her cream flooded her hand and the battery operated boyfriend so much so that it slid quicker and faster in and out smoothly as the last tremors racked her body. Sated, she lay back on the bed and smiled.

She had gone to the girl's house to find her. Jazzie wasn't home, of course, but it had been really easy to pick the lock. She'd only gone there to talk to the stupid author. Ginny snorted and glanced over at the books on her nightstand. They were all Jasmine Blackwell's and, while Ginny had enjoyed them for the most part, she felt that she could do so much better. The girl was a hack, plain and simple.

Then when she'd gotten inside, she'd gotten pissed. She had everything. Nice furniture, nice televisions, she even had all those really cool things in her kitchen that Ginny had seen in those glossy magazines. Not that Ginny would know how to use most of them, but that didn't mean she didn't want them for her own. By the time she'd gotten upstairs and saw that the man, the drunk, had his clothes everywhere she was livid. The first thing she'd torn up was his stuff.

By the time she'd gotten to the hall again and not been able to get one of the rooms open, her anger was completely out of control. She was in a rage so deep she'd completely destroyed the other rooms before she knew it. Twice she'd heard Guinevere, but she hadn't paid any attention to her. She was slipping out the back door when she heard the cars pulling into the drive. She wished now that she'd stayed long enough to see the girl's face, but her foot was throbbing again and she had to leave.

Getting up, Ginny went to the bathroom. It was there that she saw the other woman. She was surprised by her and tried not to show it. She washed her face before she acknowledged her. Then she looked at her fully after she hung her towel.

"Now what? What the hell did you expect to accomplish by destroying the house? Make her come out from hiding and let you have her killed? You're as stupid as Guinevere." That comment startled her into looking at the other woman. "You really can't be that ignorant to think I wouldn't have known about you two, did you?" Her laughter was a short bark. "You did. Oh, that's too funny."

"Who are you? And how long have you been there?" Ginny didn't like this. She wanted to control Guinevere and had a feeling this woman could control them both. "I demand that you tell me who you are."

"Demand? You're in no position to demand anything. But I will tell you. I'm Verrie. And how long…gee, I would say…I don't know, maybe forever. But at least since you started planning this disaster and watching from the sidelines while you two fucked it royally. Where do you get your ideas, from television?" Ginny flushed. "You do, don't you? Oh my, that's wonderful. You should probably go on tour after this. You could bill yourself as the idiot who couldn't think her way out of a wet paper bag."

"I'll have you know that I've everything under control. So you can just go back to where you were. I'm in charge here and—"

"And what? You'll do what to me?" Ginny felt the pain in her head. "You'll do nothing but listen. You should have more respect. I got that cat into this…this dump and neither of you were the wiser. No, you'll do well to remember that I'm stronger and I mean to stay."

Ginny was afraid of that. She'd known there were others that Guinevere had inside of her. She also knew that most of them were strong forces. But she had expected them to…well, let her control Guinevere and be glad for it. The woman laughed again and Ginny looked at her.

"You're plotting to get rid of me. Well, you can try. I'm going to run things now and there will be no more fuck-ups. First thing that has to go is that man. He is nothing but a fool. If he killed this girl and I agree, he did do it, then he'll more than likely cut a deal to save his ass if he's given a choice. And if you think giving him a few bucks will keep him from throwing us under the bus then you're stupider than I thought."

Ginny started to say something, but her head gripped in pain. She dropped to her knees and cried out in pain. Guinevere was there for only a few seconds then disappeared. The pain was incredible and her nose began to bleed. Ginny barely made it to the bed before she lost her grip. She heard Verrie laugh again as she slipped away.

~~~

Their things were put away by a very nice maid. Nathan didn't want to enjoy being there, but he did. He sat down on the bed and bounced a couple of times before settling. And Jasmine seemed to be relaxing more as she settled in. They didn't really have much. Most of what they'd brought with them was her office stuff. He'd told her they'd go shopping tomorrow.

"I guess we'll be safe here. They have a state of the art security system here." Jasmine moved around the room, touching things and straightening others. "And it was really nice of her to let me set up an office in one of the spare bedrooms."

160

"She has plenty of room, even with us staying here."
She nodded and he grinned. He wanted her. He thought
maybe if he got her under him she'd feel better too. "Come
here."

He'd put just enough command in his voice to have her
looking up. He could see her nipples pucker beneath her bra.
Nathan watched her walk toward him. "Take off your
clothes. I want to see you." His cock hardened in his pants.
Christ, this woman was beautiful. "Leave on your panties."

She'd told him the other day she couldn't wear a dress
when she worked. She said that it brushed against her legs
and it distracted her. He could see that. She had a way she
did things and breaking the habit, even as small as wearing
different clothes, could keep her from what she loved. She'd
just run out of the house to get something she needed for
reference when the break-in had occurred.

She stood before him in the tiniest little panties he'd
ever seen. And she was wet. He watched her face as he stood
up and walked toward her. Lust and need reflected back at
him. Nathan took a deep breath and could smell her arousal.
"I got us some toys. I had them in my car when I came home
tonight. Would you like for me to show you what I got?"
She nodded then answered the correct way. "Good girl. I'm
going to use them on you. One in particular I'm going to
really enjoy using on you. Would you like that?"

"Yes, Master."

He brushed his fingers over her hard nipples. "I have
some pretty clamps that I'm going to put here and make
them red for me. Then I'm going to put one on your clit. I'll
lick it first, lick it until you want to come, then I'll tighten
the little screw over you and watch as your nub gets full of
blood and swollen for me." He walked to the bedside dresser
and pulled out the box.

There were more things that he'd gotten today. Most of
those were still in his trunk, but these he wanted to play with

now. He couldn't wait until they had a home of their own, one that he could build a nice playground in. He had to adjust his cock as he dumped the clamps in his palm.

"Tell me when it hurts too much. I don't want you to be in too much pain. It won't be any fun for either of us if you don't enjoy it." She nodded and he let her not answer. He saw her swallow several times as he opened the first one up.

He took her nipple into his mouth. He sucked hard, bringing as much blood to the tip as he could. He bit her once before he laved her. He wanted to take her entire breast into his mouth, but wanted to put these in place first. When he pulled his mouth away and put the first one on her, she swayed slightly. After she assured him she was all right, he did the same to the other nipple.

She looked beautiful standing there with his clamps on her. He reached into his back pocket and pulled out the long box he'd thought to give her the other day. It was a choker. His own design that he'd had made for just her. He opened the box now and showed it to her.

"You'll only wear this when we're in the bedroom. I don't want anyone else to know what we do just yet. Not until we are more comfortable with our relationship." He had her turn as he put the gold chain on her throat. "This gold chain is especially designed for you. See how the jewels are interwoven in the circles? They had to put tiny holes in them to make them hang just the way I wanted them to." He turned her to look. "It's beautiful, as are you."

Nathan went to the bed again and picked up the two items he wanted to use on her as well as the last clamp. He dropped to his knees before her and pulled her wet panties out of his way. Her breath caught as he moved his finger along her seam. He looked up at her.

"I'm going to suckle at your clit until I get it hard. Then I'm going to put this last clamp there. Do you remember what you need to say if it's too much?"

162

"Yes," she said huskily. "Red to stop you immediately, yellow for you to slow down, and green..." He laid his mouth over her pussy and took the hard nubbin into his mouth. She cried out the words, telling him that it was a go.

He couldn't seem to get enough of her. Her taste, her body. He wanted more than anything to lay her down and fuck her, but knew that he'd never finish what he'd started. Before he changed his mind and did, indeed, take her he clamped the last one onto her and held her while she trembled. She nodded when he asked her again if she was all right.

He'd learned very quickly in his training that pain was fun. But, like too much of anything, it could be just painful. He didn't want her to be in pain, not the kind that hurt, but the kind that was rewarded with pleasure. Nathan suckled her clit again, nursing from it as he pressed his fingers over her tiny hole.

He picked up one of the two items he'd dropped on the floor while he clamped her. "Do you know what this is?" She shook her head. "It's a butt plug. I have five of them in varying sizes. This one is the third smallest. I've been stretching you for a few weeks now and know that the first two would be too small."

He watched her eyes for some sort of emotion. He wanted her to like this, but was willing to go much slower if she needed it.

"Will you put that in me? Put that in my ass to make it so that you can enter me there?" He nearly came at the greed in her voice. "Are you going to fuck me, Master?"

"Yes. I'm going to fill your tight little ass with my cock and your little pussy, my little pussy, with a big dildo. Then I'm going to fuck you hard. Would you like that, slave? Would you like for me to bend you over something and feel my cock deep in your ass?"

"Yes," she hissed at him.

He stood up and told her to go to the chair. "Put your hands on the arm rests and spread your legs. I'm going to fill your pussy, then I'm going to play with your ass. Are you ready for that?"

"Yes, Master." He waited, he knew she had something to say. "Nathan, I…will it hurt?"

"Yes. It will burn for a bit then, as the pleasure takes over, it will feel incredible. And once I fill your pussy and your ass you'll not believe how wonderful it feels."

"Have you…has anyone, have you had anyone fuck you this way?"

He had expected this question. It was something that no one knew of him. He would be honest with her even as much as it embarrassed him. "Once. It was…I was high and he wanted me. I didn't have enough sense to tell him to stop or even to not do it. He was rough and I bled for a while. I won't do that to you. I'm going to take my time with you and not hurt you, I promise."

She looked at him over her shoulder. "I trust you. More than anything or anyone I trust you. But if you don't hurry up I'm going to hurt you."

Chapter 18

She moved back to the way he'd positioned her. She was excited, nervous, but excited too. He was the man she loved and she wanted this, she was sure, as much as he did. She felt his warmth as he ran his fingers down along her spine. She shivered.

"Relax. I'm not going to do anything that I won't tell you about first. Feel my hand? I love the feel of your skin under my fingers, warm and soft." She felt herself relaxing by degrees. "I'm going to rub some cream on you. I've gotten it warm for you."

His fingers slid across her muscles and when she started to tighten up he leaned down and kissed her ass. Then he took a small nip. She moved back against his mouth as he ran his tongue up her spine. She hardly felt him as he moved up behind her and moaned when his cock, bare of his pants, slid between her legs.

"Please, Master. I ache for you." Her body didn't just ache, it burned. She wanted to beg him for more, but was afraid he'd stop. She wanted his touch, all of him.

His fingers sliding across her again had her pushing back against him. This time when he moved she felt his cock near her entrance. She didn't tense up, but relaxed against him.

"That's it, baby. I want you to bear down when I move inside of you. Relax and let me in." The slight burn turned to pleasure almost immediately. "Christ, you have no idea how badly I want to fuck you right now. I'm going to slide the dildo into you and you'll feel me inside of your pussy too.

He slid in her at both ends. She reached between her legs and felt his cock as it moved slowly inside of her. He hissed, "yes," and she cupped his balls every time he rocked into her.

She felt him pause and then she cried out when the dildo in her ass started to vibrate. "Nathan, please. Oh my God, yes."

She couldn't have stopped herself from coming if her life depended on it. She didn't care if he punished her or not. The sensation rippling through her had her screaming out his name as he slammed deep, the vibrator bringing her again and again.

She was panting as he leaned over her. She knew that he'd come, she'd felt him. It was all she could do to stay where she was, holding them both up as their breathing came out in great gasping breaths.

"I should beat your ass for that, but I can't seem to bring myself to care that you came without my permission. Hell, all I can think about now is whether or not I have the strength to stand up enough to make it to the bed, or should we just collapse on the chair and sleep here?"

She giggled. "I think the bed will be much more comfortable. Besides, I don't think I'll be able to hold you up much longer. My whole body wants to recuperate."

He kissed her shoulder. "I know. Just give me a few seconds...Christ, woman you're going to kill me. That didn't turn out the way I'd planned. Next time, and you can bet there will be plenty of next times, I'm going to have to make you come before I play so that you can hold out."

166

That made her shiver and, when he growled, she knew he'd felt it too. The thought of spending the next few hundred years with this man made her feel wonderful. She smiled when he helped her stand. They stood holding each other until he asked her if she wanted a bath.

"Yes. Oh, that would be so wonderful. I'll just be a few minutes then I'll come to bed. I've not had a bath in ages." She squealed when he picked her up. "Nathan, put me down. I must weigh a ton."

"Three," he told her with a grin. "And we're taking a bath. I want to relax too. Come on, we'll take a nice bath and then hit the hay. I've got several meetings in the morning and you have some property to find."

The bath was more than she could have hoped for. After he removed the clamps she came again with his permission and help. She couldn't believe how incredible it felt. The water was hot and Nathan washed her hair while he talked. He told her of his day and the plans he had for tomorrow. She told him of her meeting with Chastity and with Drew. By ten o'clock, they were both sound asleep in their new borrowed bed and holding each other very tight.

By the time she was leaving the house, she was running an hour behind. It had been the best night's sleep she'd had in a month and she'd not wanted to get up. Nathan had taken the covers from her and she knew she'd either have to get out of the bed or simply be chilled. Her phone ringing had her moving after a quick conversation with her publisher.

"We have that meeting at ten in the Four Seasons. Don't forget to bring your pen. We will be signing a great many contracts. Both with the production company and also with HBO. They want some things changed so is your buddy the lawyer coming along?"

"Drew, yes. He will meet us there. What sort of changes? Nothing major?" she asked as she drove through heavy traffic. "Drew told me yesterday that there are some things he wants to go over with them as well."

"Humm, let me see…one was a name change. Nothing important I think on that one. It seems one of the people on the staff had a boyfriend by that name and he died overseas in the last campaign. I would have thought that they'd like the honor, but it's that guy who gets killed at the end of this book so I told her I'd ask. The other is…I don't remember. I told Drew, he's aware of both." Jazzie heard the traffic as Chastity continued. "There is also the new cover. How do you want that one handled? Later or today when this thing is over? It's really lovely if you ask me, but…well, not enough sex. I'll let you handle that one."

Jazzie rolled her eyes. Like she cared what the cover looked like. Most of the time she just let Chastity handle that, but the last several books she'd been having a say. It wasn't that she was a prude, but she did try to have them look a little less pornographic. Not that she ever changed anything except maybe the letter coloring but she did like to be a part of it.

"We'll table that one for after. Oh, I got that invite in the mail. What do you know about that dinner thing?" Jazzie glanced over at the pretty envelope sticking out of her purse. "It says an honor, but not what sort of one."

"Invite? I'm not sure. Where from? I'm sure I would have…nope, nothing here. When is it? I'll have Mark look into it for you. And the place if you have it. I don't know anything about an honor, but you know if they are honoring my favorite author then I'm right there." Jazzie gave her the details and then she heard her talking to Mark, her husband, who helped her in the office. "He'll look into it."

"I'm nearly at the realty office now. I'm putting my house on the market. Also, if you know of anyone with some property to sell, I'm looking. But don't…well, you know. I don't want them to jack up the price because they think they can get it."

Jazzie spent forty-five minutes in the office. Her head was pounding and she wanted to strangle the man who was fast becoming her worst enemy. He'd asked her more about the place that she was selling than what she was looking for. She just knew it was a dead end. She called Nathan on her way out to the car and told him.

"Let me ask Alyssa if we can use her realtor. They work for the company in finding property and such for her to get cheap. Maybe we can get a deal. By the way, we're to meet a friend of mine for dinner. He said he wants us to come by his club. It's called Tightly Bound. Are you interested?"

She stopped walking and smiled. "Byron Grant and his wife Ta? I know them, too. Yes, that would be wonderful. I haven't seen Byr since I was a kid."

He laughed and told her he'd pick her up at the house. "I'm looking forward to taking you there and taking you." She melted under his words. "And when we build, we'll put in our own play room with all the things we like there."

"Nathan, please tell me that you want me as badly as I do you right now. If you do, I'll so make it worth your while not to work late tonight." She slid into her car. "I'm so wet right now. I'll have to change when I get back to the house before I go with you tonight. I'm sure that my panties are soaked through." She smiled when he growled at her. That alone could make her come.

"I'm going to do what I've been promising for weeks now. Your tight little ass is going to be pink when I'm finished. And as for your panties, I told you not to wear them so you'd better not be wearing any when I get home. They won't last if you do."

She made her way to the restaurant without even thinking about it after they hung up. He had her so worked up she was sure that she was driving on auto pilot. She pulled into the parking lot a whole twenty minutes early. She was just about to get out when someone knocked on her passenger window. She looked over at the woman and smiled as she rolled it down.

"You Jasmine Zinnia, the writer?"

She nodded, wondering what she could want when her window exploded near her head. She was screaming even before the door was snatched from her. And the last thing she saw before something was pressed over her face, she could swear, was her mother.

~~~

Verrie laughed when she watched Guinevere's daughter crumple to the ground. The man who she'd hired to get the daughter was throwing Jazzie over his shoulder as she made her way to the van. She glanced up at the cameras over on the next two buildings. They had been put out of commission when Verrie had found out that the daughter was coming here for a lunch meeting. It was amazing what one could do with a handgun in this state.

Fred dumped the girl in the back and Verrie smiled at him. He had asked for a hundred bucks to help with this part of the killing and now that he'd served his purpose, she drew her gun and shot him between the eyes. She simply tilted him into the back of the van beside Jazzie. The woman who had distracted Jazzie for them was already dead near the car.

Verrie went to the other body and tried to figure out if she could lift her. When she decided that she couldn't lift her on her own Verrie simply rolled her under the girl's car. It might be awhile before she was found, but honestly, she didn't care. She had just what she wanted. Of all the women who had been working on this mess she was the first to get one of the fucking brats in her hands.

It took her ten minutes of driving around to find another license plate. She looked for the same make and model van that she was driving and close enough to the same color that she wouldn't be missed for a bit. She had to abandon one for another because the screws had been so rusted that she wasn't able to get them free. Then the fucking things were expired. She was glad that she'd noticed that before she got them onto the stolen van.

Stripping off the gloves she used to get the plates, she put them in her pocket and put on another pair before she got into the van. No sense in screaming that she'd been in the fucking van, she thought with a smile. Her hair was tucked up under a hat as well. All in all it took her forty minutes to get the girl to the old house.

Leaving Fred in the van she rolled the girl out onto a tarp to drag her inside. She'd planned for this to happen and had everything she was going to need to make it as easy as possible. Another dose of chloroform kept her from waking before she was ready and Verrie threw her on the floor and tied her up. She was just getting ready to leave again when Tank showed up.

"I thought I told you to wait until I called you." She reached for her gun only to remember that she'd left it in the van. "I have this under control and I was going to call you when I had it set up."

He nodded before speaking. "I know what you told me, but I want to be a part of all of it. That was the deal I had with the other one. She knows. Ask her when you talk next."

Verrie didn't like this. He seemed to know something and, anyway, she wasn't sure she completely trusted him to…well, she didn't trust him to be a bad guy like her. She smiled to herself thinking that was the stupidest thing she'd ever thought and then went to the kitchen to find the cleaning solutions she'd left the day before. When she came back, Tank was laying out a sleeping bag. She stiffened as she watched.

"I don't want you sexually. But I'm staying here until I leave this place. There are too many things…cops are all over the fucking place just waiting for someone to fuck up and I'm keeping myself outta sight." She moved into the room as he continued. "Besides, you need to have someone watch over the girl, right? I can do that while you get whatever it is you need."

She knew this guy was supposed to be the killer, but he seemed to have this little boy idiot thing going on that she couldn't understand. She supposed that was the way he got his victims to come to him. Charm them then kill them. She'd seen his little book of wonders too.

"You can stay, but I'm not fucking carting shit around for you. You want food, you fucking will walk into town to get it or starve. I won't—" He pulled a backpack from behind the chair and started to take things out. "You knew I'd be here?"

"No. I just followed you. I also put the woman you killed somewhere else. I don't want anyone coming here either. You'd do better to hide stuff than to just let it go. 'Cause no matter how much you think you got it all, you still leave bits of you behind."

Verrie finished cleaning the girl off. She didn't want anything to bring them back on her ass; she wasn't that stupid. She wanted to ask the big man if he thought she'd missed anything, but that would be like admitting that she didn't fucking know what she was doing. She stepped back and admired her work.

There were cuts all over her face. Not that it mattered; she'd be dead in an hour anyway. The bruise to her jaw was unexpected. Verrie hadn't realized that Fred had hit her. Again, not that it mattered. She made sure the ropes were tight around her arms before she moved out of the room. Verrie noticed that Tank was asleep. She wanted to rest too, but didn't know when she was supposed to find the time. She kicked his foot as she was pulling on her jacket.

"I'm going into town. There's more knock-out shit on the table. Make sure she is always out when you're here. I want her terrified when I kill her, but I don't want her screaming her head off before I get back. You going to be here when I return?" She hoped so, but didn't comment when he nodded.

She slipped her gun in the back of her pants as she got under the wheel of the van again. She had some things to tell Ginny when she saw her next. Like not hiring stupid people for one thing and for another, she wanted her to acknowledge that she'd done what they both hadn't. She'd gotten one of the brats.

Chapter 19

Drew looked at his watch again. He didn't like this. Jazzie was really late and the girl was never late for anything. He tried her phone again and it only rang.

"Maybe she's having a nooner with that boyfriend of hers. Nathan somebody. Could be, you know. I've never seen two people more in love than those two."

Drew looked at Chastity hoping that she was right. "Nathan Howard and I don't know. I should call him and see, but I don't want to worry him if it's not necessary." He picked up his phone again and decided that he'd better, especially with all the other shit going on. "I'm going to call. What harm can it do?"

The other guests had called to say they were running late. The man, Patrick, said that there was a big to-do right around the corner from them and they had been stuck in traffic. Drew hadn't given it much thought as there was always some to-do or another going on. But Jazzie being late and not calling made him nervous. Nathan answered on the first ring.

"No. I talked to her about an hour ago," Nathan said when he'd asked if she was there. "She said she had a terrible time with the realtor, but nothing more. She's never late. Let me see if I can call her at home. Maybe she went there and is too upset to get going or something."

Drew had a sudden horrible feeling. "I'm going to call Cait. There was something going on around the corner. Maybe she's...Christ, I don't know. Call me back if you, you know, call me back no matter what."

Cait called him back. He'd had to leave a message with her dispatcher and in just a few minutes, he was speaking to her. "I was just trying to call Cain."

Drew felt as though his entire world came to a halt. He scribbled a note on the pad he'd brought and shoved it at Chastity. He nodded when she looked up at him alarmed. He started toward the entrance to the restaurant as he started barking questions at the police captain.

"We were notified by this kid that swears he saw some broad—his words not mine—pop this big fucker, again his words, in his head. He said she shoved him in the back end and closed up the doors on him. Said she screwed around in this little four wheeler before she and the dead guy took off. I've run the plates. It's Jazzie's car." Cait was talking to someone else before she continued. "They have done a thorough search and she's not here. There was a body found not ten yards from her car. And Drew...there's blood and a bloodied chloroform rag still at the scene."

He couldn't seem to breathe. He had to sit down on one of the cars that were along the sidewalk and lean over. He loved Jazzie like he would his own sister, and his wife... "Where are you right now? I'm coming there."

"It's...I suppose telling you it's a crime scene won't matter, will it? Fucking families never listen. I'm at the south lot of the Four Seasons. Do you know where that is?"

Drew slid to the ground. "I was supposed to be having lunch with her in the restaurant. She was supposed to meet me here. Fuck, what am I going to tell Cain?"

"I have an officer going to his office now. And one to Alyssa's. They won't be here for at least another twenty minutes. I thought if I had someone drive them that... What the fuck am I talking about? There isn't a man on my force that wouldn't do anything for either one of them. Shit, if I know either one of them, they are fucking driving the cruiser here themselves with my men in the back tied up. Fucking families. You're all alike. I know. I have one just like yours."

He was walking now, but not steadily. He told Cait he'd be there in a few minutes and called his wife. Quinn was already making arrangements with his granddad to come and sit for the babies. Cain had just called her. They were going to the scene en masse it seemed. Drew came up on the scene just as the coroner was pulling up. There, in the middle of the yellow tape was Jazzie's car.

He wasn't sure what to do, but he wasn't leaving. He called Nathan next who had been informed by his sister what was going on. He was frantic with need for information. Drew tried to tell him what little he knew, but the man was barely listening.

"You have to tell me it's not her body. Please, Drew, I can't live…I won't live without her. I need her. I need her so much." Drew assured him several times that it wasn't her. "Thank you. What do you know? I checked my phone records; I talked to her eighteen minutes before you called me. She said she was headed to the restaurant to meet you and her publisher. Something about a meeting with the movie people."

"Yes. That was right. I wonder if someone knew she was meeting us here today and that's why they were able to take her. She and I set this up last week so any number of people knew she was coming here, I suppose." Drew tried to remember who he'd told. Or for that matter, who he hadn't. It had been all over the paper that she was meeting with the director today. Hell, anyone from the other office to the newspaper could have told the kidnapper.

177

"I'm coming there," Nathan said. "I'm coming with Alyssa and Cain. There's a cruiser here now to…they don't think we had anything to do with this, do they?"

"No. They didn't think you guys would drive safely. Actually, I think it's a great idea. Just come here. There isn't much we can do, but maybe you can see if anything is missing from her car." Drew started to hang up when he hear Nathan sob. "We'll find her. I promise you, we'll get her back." Drew hoped so. He didn't know what he'd do if anything happened to his Quinn or their children.

~~~

Tank watched the girl. She wasn't coming around as quickly as he'd hoped, but still… He wondered what the fuck he was doing. There was no reason in the world he should be getting involved in this crap, but here he was. He shifted on the hard floor and tried to think through the women.

There was the first one, the mother. She seemed off most of the time and he wasn't so sure she even realized that she was. She could and did justify everything she did as a matter of course, and everything she blamed on the "money-grubbing whore."

Then there was the second one, Ginny. She wasn't just off, but he felt she had an unhealthy obsession with the man Cain. She hated the wife too and called her the same thing that Guinevere did, but Cain… Again, he wondered if there was something there that he wasn't seeing. Or if he ever would. Then there was the third one.

He'd seen her before when one of the women would drift away only to have her come to the surface and smile at him. Not a lot, but enough to know she was crazy. Not the kind he was, and he knew that he was off his own rocker, but this one would kill her own mother and not think anything of it. But he supposed that was what Guinevere was basically doing.

178

But this one was kill-whoever-and-fuck-the-consequences kind of nuts. She was the kind of killer that would shoot someone in front of the cops and dare them to arrest her. He'd seen her kind before. They were dangerous. He supposed that was why he was here. Control.

And that was another thing he didn't understand. Why? Why would they need the adult children dead? Didn't they realize that there were kids from these people and those kids would inherit the money? And what the fuck? Why not just, well, he didn't really understand why they didn't try to make nice with the money holders and be pissed off at them all when they were at home. People drove him nuts, more so when they thought they could get something for nothing.

As for his own dose of crazy-city, he knew that he wasn't any better than they were. He'd been a killer most of his life and didn't foresee himself changing any time soon. And if he was honest with himself, he wasn't even sure that he'd want to. He liked what he did. Tank smiled. Okay, he loved what he did. Killing got him off and he liked that sated feeling he got after it.

But his own kids? No, he knew that he'd never do that. Of course, he had killed pretty close to his own gene pool before. His brother, for one. But he'd been trying to kill him. Then there was his uncle. He'd been trying to molest Tank when he'd been a kid. Tank supposed that was his first real rush with death, the death of his uncle.

The girl moving around brought him to the present. He stood up and walked over to her. "Do you know what this is?" She nodded when he ran the knife blade across her throat. "Don't make a sound. If you do then I'll slit your throat and walk away and leave you here to rot. I'm watching you. And I want some questions answered."

When he was satisfied that she would remain quiet, he went back to his sleeping bag. She didn't seem the type to scream her head off and he was glad that she hadn't.

179

"I'm going to ask you some questions and I want you to answer them truthfully. I'll know if you're lying to me." She nodded again. "Why are you here? And don't pretend to not know what I'm talking about."

She seemed to be thinking about it. He let her. Unlike some people, he didn't feel the need to fill in the silences with fuck talk. That's the type of talk where someone just continually emptied their head and didn't say a fucking thing. Made a person want to fucking bash in their brains. He hated people like that more than anything.

"I don't...someone has been trying to kill off my family for... I honestly don't know. I have a theory if I can tell you that."

He told her she could. He admired her in that moment. She wasn't like some of his other victims because she wasn't freaking out. He supposed that was why he'd not killed her yet. She was...well, hell, he was impressed with her so far. And he found he wanted to know what she thought.

"I think it has to do with money. You see, it all started with my father. He...he was going to kill Quinn, she's my sister. He wanted to kill her because he felt that Alyssa, my sister-in-law, owed him millions. Something about finding her first. But he hadn't. Cain did."

"I thought your father was dead." He tried to remember what he'd been told by Ginny. Something to do with a ransom, but he couldn't remember right now. He thought he should have brought his notes with him too.

"He is. That's what has us all so confused. We don't... You're the man from the book signing, aren't you?" she asked him suddenly. "The one that my brother-in-law thought was going to kill me."

He nearly told her yes, but he waited. He was more and more impressed with this one all the time. He changed the subject, but thought he might come back to her question later. If he got the chance. "Then what does this have to do with him? You have any idea why you've been targeted?" He really wasn't sure of that one, but he thought maybe she didn't either. "I'm thinking it's sort of hard for a dead man to have you kidnapped and then killed."

She didn't say anything for several minutes. He knew what she was thinking. He'd seen her body stiffen when he'd mentioned killing her. But he was too wrapped up in the why and not the end result. She was going to die, there was no doubt about that, but whether from his hand or the woman who'd left remained to be seen.

"I'm in love, you know. I never thought that I'd ever want anyone to love me. I've loved Nathan for so long that I... After my father raped me, I assumed I'd...I never dreamed that someone would want me after that. I dated some, but they left me terrified by the end of the evening and I simply quit trying."

He wasn't going to be moved by her confession and shifted on the hard floor. He was going to get his answers, kill her, and probably the bitch who'd double-crossed him. Any one of them had done it and he wasn't going to be put off because they had this thing going on.

"And this man, this doper, you think he loves you? More than likely not. Men like him, they don't love, they use. And in a few years, less probably if you'd managed to get hitched to him, he'd start using again and before you know it, he's knocking the shit out of you and any kids you might have spawned and then where would you be? Nowhere. You should be thanking me. I'm saving you a world of hurt." He heard her sniffle and shifted again. "Crying is only going to piss me off so cut that shit out right fucking now."

She quieted down and he didn't ask her anything else. He wondered if she slept, but didn't think so and when she spoke again, he didn't know what to do.

"I think I'm pregnant. I know you have no reason to believe me, but...I'm late. I'm never late." He heard her sniffle again. "And I know that it makes no difference to you one way or the other, but...well, there you have it."

Yeah, he thought, there he had it.

Chapter 20

Every time the phone rang Nathan nearly went through the ceiling. He wanted her home and since no one was calling to say they had her he was thinking the worst. And the longer he had to think, the worse the scenario got. He was pacing in the kitchen when the phone rang again. He didn't even bother trying to see who it was. The cook was ignoring him anyway.

Not that he blamed him. He'd done nothing but annoy the guy since he'd been brought here. He loved Alyssa's home, but he wanted his Jasmine here with him, not all these people. And Shamus and Payton were not here either.

They'd been out looking for clues. He hated that term, but he knew what they'd meant. Shamus told him that Cait had called them in to look over a van they'd found. It had blood in the back end of it and a dead man. The dead man had been shot in the head. And she was reasonably sure that this was the same man that the kid has seen get shot and the woman they'd found some yards away had been a part of it. But they'd not been able to connect the dots yet.

"Nathan, they've just confirmed the blood in the van was the man's and some of it was Jazzie's. There isn't much of hers so they think it was from the cuts she would have gotten from the window breaking." Alyssa sat at the kitchen table and he joined her. "Are you all right? I know that's a stupid question, but I want you to know that we're doing everything we can to get her back."

"I know that. Christ, Alyssa, I'm in love with her. Not just in love, but hurt all over, heart-pounding, sick to my stomach in love with her." He got up and started to put together a cup of tea for her. He let her test the bottle of water before he poured it into the kettle. "You know I've not once thought of getting high. Not since I heard from you guys. It's always been right there all the time, the need to have a hit, a small drink, but I don't want that. I want her."

"She's made you a better person. And you've made her one too. Jazzie had this huge secret all this time and you made her show it to us." She took a sip of the tea before she looked up at him. "Tell me something, does she...you know...practice on you?"

Nathan couldn't help it, the question was so unexpected that he threw back his head and laughed. He kissed her cheek and hugged her. But he flushed when he thought of all the things they'd been doing and the things he was going to do to her. Alyssa smiled at him.

"I think I don't want to know what that smile means. You should know that Drew asked me to find you two some property. I have a few hundred acres that...well, I want to give to you." She held up her hand when he started to protest. "Listen to me first. I think Dad would have wanted you to have it. You're not the same boy that you were when he died. He'd be very proud of you. I know that I am. The place I'm talking about is the farm called Blue Skies. Do you remember it?"

He did. His father...Nathan senior had taken him and Robert out there a couple of years before his death. Nathan had been high, of course, and Robert had bitched the whole time. They'd been mushroom hunting and it was early spring. Nathan couldn't figure out what the fuck they'd been hunting mushrooms for when the store had them in abundance. Robert refused to leave the truck. Nathan had been about to give up and was kicking the leaves around with his foot when he'd seen one. He'd stopped kicking and looked at the large spongy thing in wonder when his dad came up behind him.

"That's a beauty, Nathan. Very big too. Let me show you how to pluck it without hurting it." They'd both gotten down on their knees and his dad had pulled out this beautiful pocket knife. He explained how to cut it off without disturbing the root system so that over the next few years, another one would grow to replace it. Then when they'd gotten home he and Nathan senior had cleaned it and cooked all the ones they'd found. It was by far the best meal he'd ever had up until then and probably since.

He didn't get to go the next year and sadly, the man had died the next. Nathan had been in another rehab place and hadn't even been there when his family needed him. His mom had brought him home for the funeral and to have him find the drugs needed to dope up his sister.

"I'll be honored to have it. And if you ever need it for a project or anything, I'll gladly give it back. Thanks, sis. You don't know what this will mean to us." He wiped away a tear that he felt threatening to fall. "And I want to thank you again for the faith you've had in me since...well, since I've been out."

Nathan went to the living room with her when she'd finished her tea. She told him she wanted to make a few calls and asked if he would mind keeping an eye on Connor. He was glad for the distraction. Connor was almost two, going on ten. He was the most energetic kid he'd ever seen. They were playing on the floor with his cars when Payton came in the room.

"She's on her way to the hospital. They found her...they're taking her into surgery as soon as she gets there. And I swear to you, that's all I know." Nathan scooped up Connor and held him close. "Cait didn't make it to the crime scene before they flew her out. She was talking, but not making any sense. I'm to take you there."

~~~

Jazzie woke once and threw up. The person standing next to her…was it a man? She couldn't tell, but she tried to ask them where Nathan was and they kept telling her to hush, they had her. She bit her tongue once when she felt something bump her, but she was drifting again before she could get an answer.

Lights flashed on and off for a few seconds then nothing again. She couldn't seem to hold on. She knew that she was hurting, everything about her hurt, but she was suddenly glad for that. Pain meant that she was alive and not dead. She was so glad for the not dead part.

Her mind drifted and things sort of became hazy, but she tried to focus on what Tank had told her. She had to remember what he'd told her. She promised him she would. He was bleeding she suddenly remembered and tried to reason why.

The next time she opened her eyes there was a nurse standing in front of her. She tried to ask for Nathan again, but she didn't think she'd made any kind of sound or the nurse was ignoring her. She thought it was the former because what kind of nurse ignored a patient? She closed her eyes thinking things were too bright not too.

Jazzie didn't open her eyes this time. She wasn't sure where she was, but she had an idea that she was in the hospital. The noises were muffled, but she could still hear the *ping-ping* of some machine. She tried to think, but her head hurt a great deal. She remembered Tank and her promise to him. She opened her eyes one at a time and was glad for the darkness.

"Hello," the woman said softly. "I'm Isabel. I'm your nurse. How are you feeling?" She might have made a reply to the nurse, but she wasn't sure. "I can get you something for pain, but the doctor wants to talk to you first. Can you wait?"

"Nathan." She knew this time she'd said it. Her voice sounded harsh and low, but she had heard it.

The nurse smiled again. "He's asleep over there on the couch. Would you like for me to wake him? He's been fighting it for several days now and I think he couldn't stay awake any longer." The nurse stood and wiped Jazzie's face. "I think I'll just get him for you both. Hold on, dear."

Jazzie had a thought that she didn't know where she was supposed to go, but she didn't want to waste the energy talking to her. She knew she'd feel much better when she saw Nathan.

"Hello, love. God, I've missed you." His voice soothed over her like his touch did. She tried to not cry, but it was suddenly too much. "Shush, I have you now and I'm not ever letting you go. I love you, baby, and I'm right here. Rest now, the nurse went to get the doctor and he'll want to talk to you."

She nodded and closed her eyes again. She didn't know what happened, but the next time she opened them, her room was much brighter and noisier. Jazzie could hear the voices, but nothing more. She didn't care. She was alive.

She faded in and out for a few more days. She marked the day with the changing of the guard and the whiteboard on the wall across from her. Every time she woke up, she'd look at it and would remember the date. Today marked the ninth day she'd been able to make out the numbers enough to tell what they were. She frowned at the name at the top. Damon Grant was her doctor? When had that happened?

She'd been told a few times that the police wanted to talk to her. She knew they would and she had to tell them what had happened. She also wanted to ask them about Tank. She was sure he was dead, but wanted to be sure. He'd saved her life and she knew it. Cait Grant was called at her request on the tenth day. Nathan was sitting beside her when the captain came in with Drew.

"I'm here as your attorney. If you'd like someone else that's not related to you, I can respect that. I won't like it, but I can respect it. I'm going to tell you now that I'm going to report back to the family what happened. Most of it anyway. If you don't want them to know anything, tell me before I leave and I swear to you they won't hear it from me. But they need to know as much as you'll give them." Drew sat down on one of the chairs and took out a pad of paper. "I'm going to take notes in the event you're charged with anything. You more than likely won't be, but just to be sure."

Cait sat in the other chair. "Can you remember what happened? And for the record, I'm going to be taping this."

Jazzie nodded. "I killed Tank. He was the man that was...he saved my life, but I killed him all the same. I was—"

"Jaz, honey," Drew said quickly. "Please don't confess to the nice cop that you killed someone. It makes my job much more difficult if you do that. Just tell her what happened."

Nathan squeezed her hand as she continued. "I was in the parking lot at the restaurant when this woman approached my window. She asked me what my name was."

"Did she ask you for your name or did she know it?" Cait asked. "It's important to know which. We can establish if she was a part of it or not."

"Oh. She said...she asked me if I was Jasmine Zinnia. I told her I was. Before I could say anything else, another person...a man broke my window on my side and grabbed me. He kept saying 'breathe, breathe.'" Jazzie looked up. "He was drugging me, wasn't he?"

"Yes. Chloroform. He left the cloth behind when he took you. What happened next? Where was the woman?" Jazzie frowned at Cait's question.

"I don't...maybe she left. I was too busy trying to get away from the man then nothing. I can describe her. Older, about mid-sixties, silver and black hair. It was a poor dye job because her roots were showing. She had on a floral dress that was bright green and orange. I couldn't see her shoes, but she did have a bag. It was dark blue and it hung from her shoulder as she leaned into my car. I never got a look at the man." Jazzie looked over at Drew when he stopped writing. "Did you find them?"

"Yes. They're both dead. The woman, Betsy Paxton, was dead at the scene. And Maxwell Strouse, her sometimes boyfriend, sometimes abuser, was found in a van several miles from there." Cait looked down at her notes before she continued. "What do you know of the man you called Tank? And for the record, you didn't kill him. One of my men did. Tank raised his gun to, what he'd assumed, wasfire at my officer."

Jazzie nodded. She remembered the cops coming in guns blazing. Tank had just—"He told me that he was going to let me go. He was taking off my ropes when someone came in the house and shot at us. I remember the pain...I was shot in the leg the first time then...then my back, but it was nothing like my leg. Tank rolled me under him and I felt... I think maybe he was shot too. I felt the bullets hit him when he was shot."

"Did you see who came in? Anything at all?"

Jazzie hadn't seen anything. She'd had the blindfold over her eyes then Tank had blocked her view. "He told me that there were three. He said that I had to make sure I told you that. That there are three in one and that the stronger one was 'verily.' I wanted him to explain, but he was, blood was pouring from his mouth and I knew he was dying. I don't know what he meant by that, do you?"

"No. I'm sorry, sweetie. Did he say anything else?" Cait looked over at Nathan when he cleared his throat. "You have something to say there, big boy? You're still on my shit list so spill it or I'll have to have you pulled over every time you come through town."

"No, ma'am. It's just that I was wondering if she was going to jail when she left here. Seems she's a victim, not the one who killed the man." She glared at him as he continued. "You have guards outside her room as well as checking everyone who comes in here. I just assumed—"

"You stick to your job and let me do mine," Cait told Nathan with little heat. "They're here for protection if you must know. The man who was killed by my police was Jacob Webster. His father did some time with yours. We don't believe that the senior had anything to do with the son, nor do we think that Michael Ross, otherwise known as Major, even knew he had a son. There was a daughter too, but she died of an overdose some years ago."

Jazzie looked over at Drew and then Nathan before she spoke again. "He told me…he said he was a bad man and that he'd killed a lot of people for both money and pleasure. He said that what was going on with my family wasn't right. That someone needed to be aware of what she was doing."

"She who? Did he tell you who she was by any chance?" Jazzie shook her head at Cait's question. "I wonder if he knew, himself."

Chapter 21

Cain kept an eye on his sister. He wasn't sure, but he thought she knew more than she was telling everyone. He had no idea what it could be, but he was sure something was keeping her quiet. He decided that he was taking her out to lunch today to her favorite restaurant and seeing if he could get it out of her. She'd not been out of the house since she'd been released from the hospital over three weeks ago.

"It'll be fun," he'd told her when she tried to beg off. "Besides, there are some things I need to ask you about Alyssa's birthday gift. I want your opinion on it before I give it to her."

"Cain, we both know that's bullshit. You know your wife better than she does and my opinion has never mattered one hell of a lot before. I'm fine. I'm fucking fabulous. I just wish you people would back the fuck off." She looked at the stairs and he knew she was going to go back up to her bedroom again and hide. "I'm really tired. I think I'll go and—"

"Hant J mine," Connor said as he toddled over to Jazzie. "Mine." He crawled up into her lap and handed her his favorite truck.

"He loves you very much. And I think he knows that you're sad. Tell me what's happened, Jazzie. Please? You've no idea how much we're all worried about you. You can't stop living like this."

She looked up at him while Connor took his truck and drove it over her arms and shoulders. "I'm dealing with it. Please don't pressure me. I just…I can't write. Maybe this is the end of what was a fun ride."

Cain was shocked. He'd heard her in the office they'd set up for her. Heard her in there clicking at the keys and hoped that she was working through the demons that way. He wondered what she was doing and she told him before he could ask.

"I'm writing my journal. I've never…there was never a need for one before. I seemed to be able to write whatever I wanted and it always made me feel better. Now, it's all I can do to go into the room and sit there." She gave a bitter bark of laughter. "I used to be able to write about anything and now all I can see is all the blood that was covering me. When I close my eyes, I can't breathe because I'm afraid that there's something going to happen and the blindfold is going to keep me from saving myself or someone I love."

"I can find someone you can talk to. You should probably do that anyway. I know of plenty of doctors that would—"

She cut him off. "No. I don't need a doctor to tell me that it'll pass. That this is all a product of what happened to me. I don't want someone to tell me that what I'm feeling is normal. Fuck that shit."

"Fuck, fuck, fuck." Connor mimicked his aunt and had them both burst out laughing. "Hant J laugh. Fuck, fuck, fuck."

"Alyssa's going to have a cow, you know that, right? And you're going to tell her that you taught him that." Cain took his son onto his lap when he started to get down. "Connor, that's a bad word. Mommy will beat your butt if you say that again."

Of course Connor continued to say it, several more times as a matter of fact. Cain couldn't persuade her to have lunch with him, but he did get her to agree to watch a movie with him and Connor. Alyssa was out at a woman's committee thing and the two of them had been assigned to watch the kid. Nathan was working late again.

Cain was worried there too. He'd heard them argue. Well, he'd heard Jazzie yelling. Nathan seemed to let her rant and then he'd walk away. Cain thought the two of them would work it out, but it didn't look good for either of them. He'd asked Alyssa about it several days ago and she'd told him to leave them to it.

"But she's hurting. Hell, he's hurting too. And I can't stand to see them breaking apart like this. What if he turns to drugs again or she pushes him away so much he leaves? I love them both too much to let that happen."

Alyssa sat in his lap. "He won't let her. He'll let her go just long enough then he'll pull her back. I have something to tell you, but you can't share it."

He wasn't sure he wanted to know. There was something so weird about having his wife say those words to him when he just knew that he wasn't going to like it, much less share it with anyone. He agreed.

"They play." He looked at her, confused. "You know, sex games. He's her Master and she's his—"

"Fuck, Alyssa. I didn't want to know that. Shit. Really? He ties her...you know, I don't want to know any more." He closed his eyes against the images that filtered through his mind. Not of his sister and Nathan, but of the things he'd seen when he'd been younger and looking up porn on the computer. "Why would you even know that?"

"Nathan told me. He said that he was building them a play—" She stopped when he glared at her. "Okay, he's ordering stuff and wanted to know if he could have it shipped here. He said he didn't want it sent to the house just

yet as they were still in the remodeling stages. Some of the boxes came yesterday."

Okay, he would admit today that he was interested, but not then. He wanted to see what sort of things came in the boxes, but not what his sister and Nathan did with them. He avoided the side of the garage for the three days they were there and, as of yesterday, they were gone.

~~~

Nathan stood back and surveyed his room. It was complete. He'd been working on it for over two weeks with the help of Byron and Taylor Grant and now it was finished. He smiled when Byron clapped him on his back.

"Looks good. And I can't thank you enough for the heads up on the new stuff. I think I'm going to order a few things from them as soon as I get back from this show." Byron handed the catalog that had come in the boxes to Taylor. "And remember my offer. I'm serious as they come about that."

He'd offered to let Nathan buy him out. He'd been both shocked and excited about it. The shops, Taylor called them, Tightly Bound, was doing well. Very well as a matter of fact, but they wanted to get out of it and try something different. There were several hundred of them all across the world and Nathan had been to several of them in his lifetime. The one in Columbus twice over the past several weeks to see how some of the toys he'd bought looked.

"I'll have to talk it over with Jasmine. She and I are getting married soon and we'd both have to agree." At least, he hoped they were. "I'm going to bring her here tomorrow and try to...I'm going to show her around."

"You mean bring her in line," Taylor said firmly. "She needs it. I was there the other day and she seems to be half the person she used to be. I love it when Byron gets all masterful with me. Makes me realize that I'm alive."

Nathan wasn't sure what to do with Jasmine. He sat on the big couch he'd picked out for the living room. He'd gotten them a big bed too and that was all. He couldn't seem to get her to be interested in anything anymore and he'd come up with the idea that maybe it was time she learned to obey him. He was getting desperate.

They'd made love twice since she'd been home, but she drew the line at playing. He'd not forced the idea because he, frankly, wasn't sure she was ready either. But he'd talked to her doctor a month ago and she'd told him that Jasmine wasn't doing as well as she'd hoped and suggested that she maybe should see a psychiatrist or someone that she could talk to. Alyssa had suggested that she get away, or maybe she needed someone to make her see what she's missing.

He'd told her he could do that. It had taken a great deal of embarrassing starts and stops to tell her what he was. She'd only laughed at him when he flushed to what he was sure was a bright, bright red. Then he blurted out that he wanted to order some toys. She confessed that she and Cain had some so she didn't know what he was so embarrassed about until he told her what sort of toys he wanted.

"Oh," was all she said then stared at him. "I didn't know. I thought when you said play you meant...I'm not sure what you meant. I never pegged Jazzie as a submissive person. I guess she told you then."

"No, she didn't know either. But she loves it. And I didn't force her. She just needed someone to bring out her submissive side and when I did, she fell right into it."

"First of all, duh, I never thought you'd force her and secondly, I'm reasonably sure she'd kick your ass if you tried. But as for her being a submissive, I guess it makes sense. She's always been so odd and high-strung, or so we all thought. Maybe having a Dom was just what she needs in her life."

Nathan and Alyssa talked for about another hour and he left with a spring in his step. He had planned out the room over the next several days and had visited Tightly Bound a few times too. He'd never played there, but had gone for ideas. That's when Byron had approached him with his offer to help him and the offer on the shops.

Now he had to get her there. Nathan was sure she'd come to the house and she'd agreed to do so tonight. He'd told her all about it and the things that were being done. He'd even told her about the room he was having built. She'd seemed less than interested and hadn't said anything.

The house was beautiful too. In addition to the play room there were seven bedrooms that he'd had condensed down to five for the extra two bathrooms. There was the master suite that had been remodeled some years ago and only needed new carpet, which he'd had lain last week. The kitchen was still under renovations and would be for another two weeks, but the cook he'd hired had assured him that he could cook them good meals on a hot plate and a dutch oven. Nathan assured him that he'd have a better kitchen than that and the man had laughed.

He gave her a tour of the house. She was still on crutches so he'd had to carry her up the long staircase. She'd protested, but he didn't care, he loved touching her. She told him she was impressed with how much he'd gotten done and then he carried her down to their bedroom.

The room was complete. He'd done most of the work in this room himself, wanting everything to be perfect. The big bed, four posters of solid oak, and the large dressers made him smile when she ran her finger over them. It also made his cock jump. He wanted her to caress him that way and soon. When she walked into the adjoining bathroom he gripped the doorjamb and took several breaths. He wanted her right fucking now.

When she wandered around the room to the door to their play room, he held his breath when she touched the doorknob. He was sure she wasn't going to open it and, when she took her hand away, he nearly whimpered. Then she took it firmly in her hand and turned the knob.

"Oh my," she said. "It's huge."

He walked up behind her and wrapped his hand around her. "I wanted you to see it. What do you think?"

She stiffened in his arms and he nearly let her go. Instead, he nipped at her neck and laved it with his tongue. She started to pull away and he continued to hold her. "No. You're going to do what I tell you tonight. And when we're finished in here we're going to sleep in that big bed for the rest of our lives together."

"I don't want to. I want you to take me—"

"Oh, I plan to do that. I'm going to take you hard and fast as soon as I get you naked. Go to the hump and wait for me." He let her go, hoping she would do what he'd commanded her. She hesitated just enough that he thought she was going to fight him, but she moved over to it.

The hump was just what it sounded like. It was a four-legged bar that had straps at each leg to tie the person leaning over it securely to it. He watched her as she dropped her crutches to the floor and held onto it. He knew he'd have to go slowly because of her injuries, but that didn't mean he couldn't give her a great deal of pleasure.

"Can you lean over it? If not, then we'll save this for another day." He walked up behind her and stretched her arms out from her body before he reached around the front of her and filled his hands with her breasts. "I've missed suckling these. I can feel your nipples. They're as hard a stones."

He ripped the buttons open and rocked his cock into her ass as he filled his hands with her lace-covered flesh again. This time he slid his hands beneath the material and pinched each nipple hard. Her small moan made him think he'd made the right decision.

"Lean over," he told her harshly. "And tell me your color when I get you where I want you." He was glad she'd worn the soft lounge pants. It made it so much easier to strip them from her. When she stood in front of him in her torn shirt, bra, and panties, he took off his own clothes. His cock was straining and leaking with need.

He helped her lean over and he moved her legs toward the posts. He wrapped the soft Velcro around her ankles and then around her wrists on the other side. She told him "green" when he'd asked her.

Her ass was so beautiful that he moved behind her again and squeezed it in his hands. He rocked his cock between her thighs and could feel the cream that covered her. He moaned when she rocked back toward him.

Nathan stepped back and brought a hand down hard on her ass. She moaned. Christ, he was going to die right now. He spanked her three more times in varying strengths until her entire ass was bright red.

"Do you know why I punished you, slave?" He didn't wait for a reply, but smacked her twice more. "When I told you to come to the hump, you hesitated. Are you supposed to make me wait when I give you an order?"

"No, Master," spilled from her mouth on a moan. "I'm to do what you tell me without waiting for you to explain. I'm sorry, Master."

He spanked her again. Then he leaned down and ran his tongue over the heated skin. Taking a small nip he asked her a color and got the same go color.

He needed to fuck her. It had been too long and he was too hard. He fisted his cock and slid it just to her entrance. She rocked back against him and moaned. He wanted to punish her, even thought he should, but his own need was too great. He slammed deep and came.

He rode her hard through his release. Grabbing her hips he threw back his head as he filled her. He felt her tighten around him and vaguely heard her own cry of release. He didn't care. He was where he needed to be.

He leaned over her, still breathing hard, and kissed her damp skin. She shivered beneath him and he felt his cock tighten. He sat up and moved into her heat again. Christ, he was hard.

"Nathan, I need... Please, red. Please, just for a bit, red."

He stopped immediately. After unstrapping her, he picked her up into his arms and took her back to their bed. He laid her down gently and covered her up and then crawled in beside her. She closed her eyes and he brushed at the tears on her cheeks.

"I didn't meant to hurt you, love. I didn't even—"

"It's not that. I thought I was dead and I couldn't...I love you so much, Nathan, and all I could think about was you getting hurt. I knew that this person was going to kill me and...and..." She burst into tears and he pulled her into his arms as she continued. "Tank told me he was going to kill me and then take my picture and show it to his potential jobs. He said that he had hundreds of them and I'd just be another footnote in his list of accomplishments. But I didn't believe him. He was too nice, too kind to me."

He held her and didn't speak. He wasn't sure what he could say to her. Cait had told him that the man Tank had saved Jasmine's life by rolling over her. But he'd raised his gun against a cop and that was what had gotten him killed. She sobbed a bit more before she starting talking again.

"I told him I was pregnant or at least I thought I was. We've never used much in the way of protection and he didn't say anything. I did really believe that I was. Actually, I had hoped up until then that I was." She pulled away and looked up at him. "I want a baby, Nathan. Yours and mine. Can we? Would you like to have a baby with me?"

He kissed her before answering, so overwhelmed with emotion. "More than anything in this world I want to see you huge with my child—our child." He rolled her to her back and entered her. "Let's get started on that right now." Her giggle made his heart soar and he smiled. She was going to be just fine.

~~~

Ginny screamed again. These fucking kids had to die and she was sick to fucking death of screwing with them. She was beginning to think there was some force against them in taking them out. Verrie had one of them so close and that fucking Tank stepped in and got all herolike on them. Ginny kicked the book across the room and dropped to the floor.

"You'd do better using your energy helping me pack. We have to leave now if we're going to hide out. I, for one, am not staying around to wait for the police." Ginny looked up in the mirror at the shadowy person there. Guinevere.

"Fuck you. You think that the fucking bastard told anyone? He would have had to give himself up if he'd done that. Get real. I vote we don't go anywhere."

Ginny continued to stare at Guinevere until she came into focus. There was always a blur between them when they spoke, but today it was harder. Then the shadows became more defined and then there was Verrie.

They were three. Ginny hadn't known about Verrie and, apparently, neither had Guinevere. Guinevere might not have still known about her. She seemed to think that they were separate people, not all in the same body. Ginny had only discovered it one day when one of the others, a childlike person, had come out and explained it to her. She'd never been able to get the childlike person's name and soon after, she never came out again.

The mirror had been a surprise as well. Guinevere had been sitting at the vanity in her room one afternoon and Ginny had just moved to speak to her. Seeing what she looked like, or she supposed what she thought she should look like, had been a surprise. She was as different from Guinevere and Verrie as they came.

Ginny was tall and thinner than Guinevere, at least in the reflection. Her hair was a dark red, almost a copper color that seemed to sparkle when she was in the mirror. At the times when she owned the body, which was more and more lately, she could see her reflection staring back at her instead of Guinevere's. Her clothes were different too. She tended to wear things that were bright and fit the form that she saw in the mirror. She'd often wondered what Guinevere thought when she came back to her own self and saw the clothes that she didn't know, or if they too were a part of what she wanted to see.

Then there was Verrie. She was older. Much older, as a matter of fact. Her hair was grayed, almost silver, and she was very heavy. Not rotund or anything like that, but she was big. And there was something simply not right about her. Ginny laughed. Like she was the least bit sane. She was sitting on the floor having a conversation with her other self in the mirror and wondering about clothes.

Ginny looked up again and saw Verrie glaring back at her. She wasn't afraid of her anymore. She'd figured out that the pain in her head was something she could control. It was there, but she could control it.

Verrie tisked at her. "You should listen to Guinevere. If we left town now we could go to New York and check out the other daughter. She won't have all this family around to get her ass out of deep water. It would also do us some good in that we can get out more as ourselves."

There was that. She had to go out and behave. If she went where no one knew her, she could simply be who she

201

wanted and fuck the other two. She didn't answer right away. There was no reason to give in so quickly.

"And you've got it all wrong, by the way."

Ginny waited for her to elaborate. When she didn't Ginny got up and starting throwing things in a trash bag, ignoring her for the moment.

"Don't you want to know?"

Ginny turned to look at her, her face sharp and in complete focus. "Know what? That we should have given up on this long ago. I'm not. I'm in this now for the money and I'm not fucking giving up."

Verrie laughed. It was hard and sharp. Ginny felt it, the pain of the laugh, and shuddered from it. When she spoke again Ginny felt herself pale and then she faded too.

"You're the real one."

About the Author

I woke up one morning and decided to give play time to the people in my head who were keeping me awake. Little did I know that they would be so relentless and want their time right now! I wrote for the pure joy of it and to entertain my family and friends. But mostly it was to get more than an hour of sleep without a story playing out. Of course, the more I write, the more they want. So...well, as a result of sleepless days (I work through the night as a gun toting grandma – nope not a vigilantly but an armed security guard) I have lots of stories written.

Hello! My name is Kathi Barton and I'm an author. I have been married to my very best friend Sonny for at times seems several lifetimes – in a good way, honey. And together we have three wonderful children and then the ones we brought into the world - Paul and Dale Barton, Jason and Wendy Barton and Danielle and Ben Conklin. They have given us seven of the greatest treasures on Earth. They don't live at home seven days a week! No, seriously, seven grandchildren – Gavin, Spring, Ben, Trinity, Sarah, Kelly and Kian.

www.ingramcontent.com/pod-product-compliance
Lightning Source LLC
Chambersburg PA
CBHW020622180626
46810CB00007B/2899